Josh's Dream

Heroes of Wolf Creek
Book Four
By
R. J. Stevens

Cover Art: SelfPubBookCovers.com/ VonnaArt

ISBN : 9798375786759
Printed in America

Dedication
To Monika
Thank you for your love and support.
You are amazing.

Prologue

Jillian Taylor anxiously drove toward her new home in Wolf Creek, Wyoming, leaving the life she lived in Arkansas behind. The dreams she held close to her heart were about to come true. Finally free from her abusive husband, she made the decision to move without telling anyone. Even her closest sister, with whom she shared everything, didn't know.

Weary of driving, she stopped at a motel off the interstate in Oklahoma for the night. There was no sense in wearing herself out. In the morning she would continue the long drive at her own pace. Her ultimate goal was to live her life on her own terms no matter what anyone thought about it. Nothing would stand in the way of the enjoyment when her dreams became reality.

***

Josh Wolf accepted the promotion he had worked so hard for. For most of his adult life, he dreamed of helping people like his oldest brother, Will, but he had no desire to join the military. Especially when he witnessed firsthand how it affected his brother.

With the help of Will's friends, he learned how to handle himself in most every dangerous situation he might find himself in as a deputy. He and James Smalley joined the county sheriff in the small police department several years ago. When his boss, Joe Dodson, needed someone to investigate certain crimes, he discovered Josh had a gift of finding even the tiniest details at a crime scene. Josh attributed this ability to his brother and his friends.

When the town counsel created the position for a detective, Joe chose him to fill that role. He vowed to be the best detective he could for the developing town. With that accomplishment, his dream turned to finding a wife and building a family with her. Although he was a patient man, he longed for what his brothers had found in the women they married.

Chapter One

Soft music drifted over the fields into the cool night as the sun sank behind the mountains surrounding the tiny community of Wolf Creek, Wyoming. An eerie silence fell over the fields.

The nightly sounds of nature were unusually quiet as though it held its breath for a coming storm.

A malevolent figure lurked nearby in the shadow of the forest, full of hatred and fury, watching, waiting. The happy friends were completely unaware of the eyes glaring through binoculars. The bitter man vowed retribution for those he held responsible for ruining his life.

***

"Congratulations!" Will Wolf slapped his brother Josh on the back.

"Thanks," he said with a smile. It had been hard to do, but he finally became the first official detective in the Wolf Creek Police Department.

The Wolf brothers sat around in Frank and Ginger's back yard enjoying the surprise party for Josh.

Josh stood up and cleared his throat and said, "Uh... I'd like to thank y'all for coming out to help me celebrate my promotion. It's been a long hard road to get here, and I have y'all to thank for supporting me. Even the few that knocked some sense into me when I wanted to quit," he let his eyes rest on Ginger. "Some of you literally knocked me in the head."

Laughter rippled through the small crowd when Ginger blushed. "Hey, that was an accident."

"Maybe, but it was effective." Josh chuckled. "Anyhow, I vow to do my best for y'all. Now let's party!"

The celebration continued until the youngsters running around the yard got cranky signaling it was their bedtime.

"Before y'all leave, thanks again." Josh said around the lump forming in his throat. "This was a great party."

Ginger hugged him and said, "You're welcome. I'm so proud of you."

"Don't give him a bigger head than he already has." Trace teased while holding his wife, Star, close to his side.

"You're the only one who needs his ego deflated once in a while, Twinkle Toes." Will laughed.

"Hey! That's not true." Trace retorted as he smiled at his wife. "Besides, I'm too happy to worry about my ego."

"Why is that?" Shadow, Star's brother, asked waiting for him to confirm his suspicions.

"Star and I are gonna be parents in a few months." Trace said with a huge smile.

"Congratulations!" the few family and friends shouted in unison.

"Let us know if you need our help Star." Ginger and Samantha offered.

"Thank you, I will." Star agreed.

After one last toast, the crowd broke up and left for their homes.

***

Josh admired his new name plate on the door to his office. He sat down behind his new desk and fired up his laptop. While it booted up, he looked around, thankful he was realizing his dreams.

He understood that in the slow periods he would be out on patrol like the others in the station. He also didn't want to borrow trouble by wishing a case would fall into his lap first thing this morning.

Sheriff Joe Dodson stepped into the doorway, "How do you like your new office?"

"To tell you the truth it's exciting." Josh replied with a smile.

"Good. I have an assignment for you." Joe said grinning as anticipation filled Josh's face. "Artie called and said someone shot at the livestock at his place. He said a bullet grazed one of his prize-winning broncos."

"I'm on it." Josh grabbed his hat moving to leave.

Joe smiled as he watch Josh stop to tell Kimberly to radio him if needed then leave the building. He wished he could go back in time to his first day as an officer. Over the years, the excitement waned as he got older. Once again he thought about retiring, but he still had a few years to give to the town he loved.

***

Josh drove past the abandoned Anderson ranch on his way to Artie's. His mind wandered back to the night a crazed grizzly bear killed Tommy Anderson. A few days later while hunting the bear, the beast nearly took the life of his own brother, Trace.

That night Joe chose him to break the news to the family. It was the first time he informed a family their loved one had died. For months it bothered him, but the angst he felt was slowly dissipating.

When he stopped at the crossroads, he noticed the stop sign riddled with bullet holes. Putting the truck in park, he got out to investigate. After a short search he found the shotgun shells he was looking for.

Quickly stashing them in his truck, he continued to the Billings Ranch.

Artie stepped out of the barn upon hearing a truck park in the drive. With a wave, he met Josh halfway to the barn. "Hey, Josh. Are you here about the shooting?"

"Yes. If you don't mind I'd like to take pictures of the injuries your horse suffered." He replied shaking his hand. "Did you hear anything before you discovered your horse had been shot?"

"No. My guess is they were too far away, and I most likely was asleep." Artie said leading him to the stall where the injured horse recuperated.

After taking pictures of the wound that Hank, the county veterinarian, had neatly stitched, he listened as Artie gave him the information on the horse and when he discovered the wound.

Shortly after he left and turned his truck toward Wolf Creek, he made a quick stop by the Anderson Ranch to be sure there were no squatters on the property. When he found everything secure, he continued on his way to the station.

Joe looked at the evidence while his new detective dusted the shells for fingerprints. When he finished, he pulled the print file to see if they could find a match.

"Looks like Brent Foster's at it again." Josh informed Joe.

"Go pick him up." Joe insisted. "Take James with you."

Josh drove out to the Foster ranch with James riding shotgun. After parking the truck, Josh made his way to the front door of the large farmhouse. He knocked waiting patiently for someone to answer while James stood near the edge of the porch.

"Hello, Detective Wolf." Mrs. Foster greeted them. "What's Brent done now?"

"I need to take him in, Mrs. Foster." Josh replied. "He's been shooting at Artie Billings livestock."

"I don't think he's had time to do something like that," she said turning to leave. "Since Harry's out working a second job, Brent's been taking care of the ranch."

"Would you like me to come with you to fetch him?" Josh offered.

"No," she declined before yelling for Brent to come downstairs.

James was ready when they heard the back door slam, and he ran around the side of the house tackling Brent before he could get to the barn.

"Stop struggling Brent!" James yelled as Josh helped him cuff the young man.

"I ain't done nothin! Let me go!" he bellowed.

When they had him cuffed and in the truck, Josh explained to his mother she could pick him up at the new station.

Brent argued the entire way back to town and struggled even harder until they got him in a cell.

"Brent stop it right now!" Joe got his attention. "You keep it up and we'll make you stay a few days."

"I ain't done nothin!" he bellowed again.

"We've got the evidence that says otherwise." Joe insisted. "Now sit down and be quiet!"

"What evidence?" he growled.

"We have empty shotgun shells with your prints on them." Josh told him.

"Someone stole my gun three days ago!" he shouted."

"Why didn't you report it?" Joe asked.

"I ain't had time. With pop working an extra job to ease the money stuff, I've been taking up the slack at home. I promise I didn't have nothin to do with whatever happened!" he claimed his innocence.

Joe slammed the access door to the cells and stomped to his office.

"Joe?" Josh followed and asked sensing something was wrong, "What's going on?"

"Archer McKinley called just before you got back to let me know Melody committed suicide last night. She couldn't deal with what that lowlife Falcon and his friends did to her."

"Man, that stinks." Josh commented. "How's Archer taking it?"

"Not well, he was going to ask her to marry him when he found another sheriff to take his place," he told him.

"Do you need to go be with your friend?" Josh asked concerned.

"Yes, I'll be back in a few hours. Hold the fort," he grabbed his hat and left.

A few days later after Melody's funeral, Joe returned to work. Josh had discovered that Brent was in fact innocent when he caught three teens new to the area with Brent's shotgun.

Bernard, Preston, and Reginald Alexander, triplets born into a ridiculously wealthy family, had moved with their parents to one of the bigger ranches east of Wolf Creek. Josh obtained a long rap sheet from the NYPD on the three troublemakers.

"Those boys have been mighty busy." Joe said with a low whistle while thumbing through their files.

"Judge Odom is gonna have a field day with them that's for sure." Josh told him.

"Give all this to our new district attorney. We'll see how well she does with her first case." Joe said handing the file back to him.

11

"Will do. I'll see you after lunch." Josh gathered the documentation and left for the new city hall.

As he walked down the street, he was still amazed at how much things had changed in Wolf Creek in the last few years. The tiny town went from having one four way stop to three. The side streets were filling up with new homes and businesses. He stepped into the court offices and found the new DA working on her computer.

"Hello, Miss Gunn, may I come in?" Josh stood in the hallway.

"Sure, have a seat, and please call me Charlotte," she waved him in. "What can I do for you, detective?"

"I have a case for you," he handed her the small box of evidence, and the file folder. "Some new kids in town have been causing trouble. They stole Brent Foster's shot gun and have been shooting up the countryside.

"Are they still in jail?" she asked flipping through the evidence file.

"Yes," he replied. "Joe told their parents the judge had to set bail before he would release them."

"They will be arraigned at nine a.m. on Monday," she replied.

"Sounds good," he said making a note in his notepad. "Have you had lunch yet?"

"No, I was just about to go find something in the little breakroom," she smiled.

"Let me buy your lunch at Ginger's, I mean Wild Mustang Bar & Grill." he insisted. "I hate that the owner changed the name."

"Oh? What was it called before?" she asked curiously grabbing her purse.

"Ginger's Bar & Grill. Ginger is our neighbor and it got too confusing when we wanted to go to Ginger's, sometimes we meant her house and not the bar," he explained as they walked across the street. "To the home folks, it'll always be Ginger's."

"Change is sometimes hard to accept," she commented as he opened the door for her.

Larry watched Josh lead the gorgeous new District Attorney to his usual table and he hurried to take their order. What he wouldn't give to be on a date with her. The minute the mayor, Will Wolf, introduced her at the town council meeting, his mind went blank. The woman was perfection in motion with her long brown hair, gray eyes, and long shapely legs. Yes, he was totally in love with her, especially when she smiled with those rose-colored lips.

"What can I get you today Josh?" he asked barely looking his direction.

"One special and a cup of coffee." Josh answered hiding his amusement.

"What can I get for you, Miss Gunn?" he asked with a nervous smile.

"I'll have the chef's salad and iced tea please." she replied smiling up at him.

"Coming right up." he said before leaving to put their order in.

"So how is your new job treating you?" Josh asked.

"Good, it's a nice change from Chicago. It was time for me to move on," she said.

"I sense there was a problem there," he replied.

"You're good," she said with a sad smile. "I had a problem with a co-worker that wouldn't leave me alone. I never encouraged him, and the boss eventually fired him. Then he started harassing me with phone calls and showing up everywhere I went. When he showed up at my home, I snuck out of town and moved here."

"Well, he won't bother you here," he promised. "We've had several stalker types come through here and we know how to handle them."

"That makes me feel a bit better," she said as Larry brought their orders."

They ate and talked about work, and Josh regaled her with stories of growing up in Wolf Creek.

After seeing Charlotte back to her office, Josh returned to the station and sat down at his desk with nothing much to do. He stood to go on patrol when Joe told him that Old man McMurphy fell and broke his hip. Doc wanted him to go see to his three milk cows and his old donkey. Grateful for an assignment, he agreed and left to help the old man out.

Chapter Two

Jillian Taylor shoved the last of her suitcases in the back of her little blue car and closed the hatch. She didn't feel a bit of remorse for leaving the husband she had just buried behind. The minute he passed away she paid to have her name changed from Pope back to her maiden name.

Deep down she wanted to tell her family she was moving across the country to Wyoming, but they would try to stop her. Since she was the youngest, they tried to run everything in her life until she met Terry. The smooth-talking city slicker, as her brother called him numerous times, fooled everyone, except him. She could have strangled him at the funeral dinner when he made his opinion of the man known. Jeb Taylor definitely had his opinions and wasn't afraid to voice them to anyone who would listen.

Embarrassed wasn't even close to how she felt when he opened his pie hole, as her uncle Jonah called it. A small chuckle slipped from her lips thinking about how he had defended her right to live her life as she saw fit. Jeb was angry at him, but Jonah defended her choices even if she made mistakes.

Two weeks after she turned twenty years old she married Terry. Three long years had passed since she gave voice to the words, "*I do*." Every night since then, she lived with his abuse.

Relief allowed her to breathe again after the initial shock of Terry wrapping his car around a tree while driving drunk.

Her family suspected the man was abusing her, but they had no idea of the life he forced on her. Parts of their marriage would haunt her for the rest of her life. It would be a long time before she would even consider dating again, let alone contemplate marriage to anyone.

Jillian went back inside to make sure she hadn't missed anything. The house and furnishings would go to Terry's little sister, Beverly, who had been the only bright spot in Jillian's life during her short time with her brother.

After she went through the house room by room, she laid the extra set of keys to the house on the table by the door and left with a sense of relief that this chapter of her life had closed. Now she had an exciting new life to look forward to away from her painful past.

Starting the car, she checked her mirrors and backed out of the driveway. Turning right at the end of the street, she began her journey into the unknown.

***

Thunder and lightning lit up the dark sky as worn windshield wipers fought to keep up with the deluge of rain pounding the old green Plymouth. Fog collected on the inside of the window while the heater struggled to put out warm air. The frail woman desperately clung to the steering wheel trying to see the muddy road in the dim light cast from the barely lit headlights.

Then a large deer leapt from the field and stopped in front of her car. Her reaction was sluggish, yet she managed to miss the animal. Sadly, the car went into a spin landing against a tree caving in the driver's side of the large car. Tears slipped down the woman's weary face as she managed to scoot across the car to get out the passenger's side.

Cold rain instantly soaked through the thread bare coat she wore. She picked up her small satchel and crossed the flooded ditch to the road. For a few moments she gazed at her car, then looked both ways unsure which direction to go. Finally, lost somewhere in Wyoming, she picked a direction to begin walking.

It seemed like she walked for hours but her worn-out watch showed it had only been thirty minutes. With each step she took, she prayed to find someone who would help her. Fear that she was in labor kept her going. Relief eased the apprehension squeezing her chest when she spotted a driveway across the road. Desperate to find help, she hurried down the old drive.

The dark house stood strong against the stormy night. After knocking several times, she realized no one lived there. She moved around to the back of the house to find it locked as well. Unable to stand the pain in her back any longer, she broke the window and unlocked the door letting herself inside.

Anxious to get warm, she found the house completely empty with the exception of curtains left behind. Shucking off her wet clothes, she wrapped herself in one of the two curtains she yanked from the window and sat down against the wall shivering. Then the pain hit stronger than before and she felt the warmth of her water breaking. Her baby was a month too early and she had no one to help her.

Fear gripped her heart as she felt the need to push. A few minutes later she held her newborn baby girl in her arms, when she felt the need to push again. Her second baby girl entered the world crying. Gently wrapping them in the other curtain to keep them warm, she leaned against the wall to feed them their first meal.

Her vision became cloudy as she gently laid them together and cuddled them close giving them the warmth of her failing body. Placing a soft kiss on her children's heads she prayed,

"Dear Lord in Heaven,
Please watch over my baby girls. Send someone to love
them like I would have.
Amen."

With a last stuttering breath, she orphaned the two tiny babies in an abandoned farmhouse in the middle of nowhere.

***

Jillian drove the muddy road toward the house she purchased with some of the life insurance money Terry left her.

Following the directions from the car's GPS, she came upon the scene of an accident. An old green car sat wrapped around a tree on the side of the road. She got out and checked for the driver but found it empty. Going back to her car, she called the police to report the accident, then continued following the GPS to her new home.

Finally, the driveway appeared and she turned and followed it until she saw the large farmhouse. There was a big red barn and small corral off to the side of the home. Parking her car and shutting the engine down, she took a deep breath as the grip of her past fell away. No one except the realtor knew she was here.

When she got out of the car, keys in hand, she heard what she believed to be kittens crying until she stepped onto the porch. That sound wasn't a kitten, that was a baby. Hurrying inside, she found the woman covered with a curtain. The bundle beside her moved with angry cries echoing in the room. Quickly pulling the curtain back, she found twin girls not more than a few hours old. The mother's lifeless eyes stared ahead. Jillian checked for a pulse, but it was obvious by the stiffness of her cold body she was dead.

Without moving the babies, she tucked the curtain around the little ones and hurried out to her car. She called the police again to inform them of what she found. Then she opened her trunk and grabbed her suitcase and emergency first aid kit. Running back inside to care for the orphaned children.

Wrapping each child in the towels she dug out of her suitcase, she put them back by their mother, forgetting the door was open. When Josh stepped inside startling her, she screamed.

"Who are you and what are you doing here?" he asked as Joe and Doc followed him.

"I'm Jillian Taylor." She said breathing heavily. "I just arrived and found this."

"Why are you here?" Josh asked with a furrowed brow.

"I purchased this ranch last week." Jillian replied tersely feeling an intense dislike of the man.

"I'll have to verify that." Josh said. "Meanwhile, do you know this woman?"

"No, I've never seen her before in my life." Jillian shook her head.

"Josh, I'll call Ginger and ask if Frank can bring the car seats they use for the boys." Doc said. "Just guessing, I'd say the woman has been dead about three hours. The babies are healthy, but hungry."

Jillian cuddled one of the little ones while Josh held the other until Frank drove up.

"Hey." He said getting out grabbing a big diaper bag from the back seat and opening the back of the SUV.

"Thanks for coming to help out." Joe shook his hand. "Hi Kevin."

19

Kevin Bright Sky acknowledged him then asked what happened. Frank took the child Josh held so he could go inside with Kevin and Joe. He then cleaned the little one and put a diaper on her. It was a tad too big but it worked for now. After wrapping the child, he traded children with Jillian and handed her a bottle. It didn't take long to repeat the process until both little ones were quietly sleeping in the car seats.

After Frank and Kevin left, Josh stayed to make sure there was no foul play while Doc examined the woman's remains.

"It looks like she died at around four a.m. according to her liver temperature." Doc informed them. "Did she cut the cord?"

"No, I did. I had to so I could wrap them up." Jillian said as Josh grimaced.

"You've cut a cord before?" Josh asked at his boss when he chuckled.

"More than once. You forget we live in a small town and how long I've been sheriff." Joe laughed.

After they transferred the woman into a body bag and placed it in Doc's truck, Josh found a piece of plywood and fixed the window in the back, then interrogated Jillian.

"Where are you from, Miss Taylor?" he asked watching her closely.

"I'm from Arkansas." She replied. "I can give you the realtor's phone number if you wish."

"Thank you, I would. Now, why would you want to live out here by yourself?" he asked. "Or do you have family coming to live with you."

"That is of no concern of yours if I'm not breaking any laws." She scowled.

"You do know there are other homes for sale just on the outskirts of town." He suggested. "You would be much safer there."

"Thank you but no." she declined. "Is there anything else detective?"

"No, but I'll be in touch after I talk to your realtor." He said and left.

Jillian was angry he seemed set on prying into her life. He might be the best-looking guy she'd ever met, but he also made her nervous. From past experiences, she learned the hard way to be cautious around such men.

Chapter Three

Josh dumped the satchel he retrieved from the farmhouse on his desk to go through its contents. A well-worn wallet held two dollars and a driver's license. Next was an empty bottle of pre-natal vitamins. Other than that, there was nothing important. Before going through the suitcase, he ran her license through the DMV but found it was a fake.

He opened the suitcase to find a few thread bare items of clothing and very few toiletries. Removing the clothes to catalog them, he noticed a tear in the lining. Carefully pulling the material back, he found an envelope. Gently opening it he retrieved a tear-stained letter that read:

J.

I'm writing to inform you that you are on your own. I never intended to enter into a serious relationship with you. You were just a way to occupy my time while I was in town. It was my hope that you knew how to keep from getting pregnant. What could I expect from a backwater hick like you? I want nothing to do with you or that child. I was only in town for a few weeks and I fully intend to leave as soon as possible. By the time you receive this, I'll be back in my home enjoying the peace and quiet again.

I've enclosed some money for you to get rid of the kid or not. There will be no more money as you have no idea who I really am. Have a nice life.

D.

Fury filled Josh as he finished the letter. How could someone do that to another person and the child, or in this case children?

Carefully dusting the envelope and letter for fingerprints, he tried to understand the situation. If it were him, he would have done the right thing. Of course, he'd only been with one girl in his life. She moved away from Wolf Creek when her parents divorced. They hadn't had any contact with each other since.

He lifted two sets of fingerprints off the envelope and one set off the letter. Instinctively he knew the second set would be the mail carrier's prints. He still looked at the file of prints they kept for Wolf Creek knowing they wouldn't be there.

Joe stuck his head into the room, "Did you find anything?"

Josh gave him the letter to read while he returned the contents of the suitcase into the evidence box.

"Man, that stinks." Joe shook his head. "If we find this guy I'm gonna make sure Judge Odom throws the book at him."

"The bigger part of that statement is "IF." Josh replied.

"It's time for you to head over to the courthouse for the Alexander triplets arraignment." Joe reminded him. "I'm headed over to testify in Ethel and Sadie's arraignment too.

The two men left together discussing the little babies that were currently in Ginger and Frank's care.

***

Ginger and Samantha sat in her den feeding the hungry baby girls. Dev, Frankie, and Willie were playing nearby in the playpen. They finally mastered sitting up on their own but hadn't figured out how to stand yet. Suzy quietly played on the floor next to them with her baby doll.

"I sure wish we could name them." Ginger said patting the little one's back to burp it.

"You still can. They're small enough they'll not remember if whomever winds up with them changes it." Samantha put the bottle in the baby's mouth. "Has Josh said anything?"

"Nothing other than it was still early in his investigation. I wish we could just go before Judge Odom and he declare us their parents." Ginger sighed.

"If only life were that easy." Samantha said. "Where's Frank?"

"He drove Elysa to the airport." Ginger replied. "They're still fighting about this new job she's taken. Elysa is adamant that she's safe with this Marty character, but Frank is worried."

"I'm sure Elysa knows what she's doing." Samantha laid the little girl down and picked Dev up to put him in his car seat."

"I'm concerned too. They're going to talk to homeless people around the country." Ginger looked at her friend with clouded eyes. She remembered the three homeless men attacking her when she ran away from Frank. "Some of those people suffer from mental illnesses. She swears Marty will protect her."

"Sometimes we have to let those closest to us figure things out on their own." Samantha said.

"I know. But Sam if anything happens to her it will devastate Frank." Ginger replied.

"I'm sure she'll be fine, just remember to pray for her every day." Samantha put a comforting hand on her shoulder. "I need to get back, Will is out riding with Spencer. I suspect he's getting anxious to go riding alone. I don't know what's bothering him the last few weeks, but I'm starting to worry about him."

"Frank is acting the same way. I wonder what's going on with them." Ginger said.

"I'll see you tomorrow at church." Samantha said and closed the door behind her as she left.

Ginger cuddled the little one before laying her in the bassinet. A short prayer slipped from her lips:
Dear Lord,
Please allow us to adopt these little ones. I've already fallen in love with them.
***

"Will? Is Josh there? Mr. McMurphy called about some kids shooting a gun out at his place." Joe said when he answered the phone.

"He's outside waiting for me to saddle my horse. We're going riding."

"Could you let him know?" Joe said. "I'll call James to help him."

"Sure." He said then hurried outside to tell Josh.

Josh kicked his horse into a run steering the horse toward his neighbor's home.

James parked his truck in front of the suspects Humvee. The boys spotted him when he got out and scattered. James chased Bernard down while Josh rode after Reginald. Using the rope he had on his saddle, he made short work of roping the young man and immobilizing him.

James took Reginald off his hands and Josh went after Preston. Worry settled over him when he saw Preston run down Will's driveway. Samantha was outside with the babies when he left.

Will stepped out of the barn with his horse when he saw some kid waving a gun shouting at Josh to stay away. Without a thought his old military training kicked in. Seconds later he disarmed the kid and had him on the ground.

"Are you hurt Samantha?" he turned to check on his family.

"Just scared." She tried to remain calm in front of the babies who huddled next to their mother.

"Thanks for taking him down Will." Josh said, "Can I leave my horse here? James has his brothers cuffed in his truck."

"Who the heck is this kid?" Will asked still seething with anger.

"A delinquent from New York." Josh said hauling the kid to his feet. "Come on, don't give me anymore trouble."

He made the kid get into the Humvee he would impound and followed James to the station.

Chapter Four

Jillian stretched on the pallet she had made on the floor, and her body let her know she needed a bed to sleep on.

Quickly dressing, she hurried outside to her car. She pulled out the list she needed to accomplish before nightfall. The first item was get some breakfast and a hot cup of coffee.

While she drove to town, she mentally ticked off the most important items. The first item on that list was trading her little car for a truck. Living on a small ranch she would need to be able to haul things, like a new bed. Although she had plenty of time to furnish the house, she was anxious to settle into her new life.

Jillian was grateful to the Lord, that between her ex-husband's life insurance policy, the trust fund she hadn't touched, and her share of her parent's life insurance policy, she had more than enough to live on for several years. If she was careful, she could stretch it for the rest of her life. Now she could work on the dream she always wanted to pursue. She would have to talk to someone about permits and such to set it all up.

When the small town appeared in front of her, she slowed to the speed limit on the sign. She stopped at the first of three stop signs. Turning right, she spotted a donut shop and a small diner offering breakfast. In need of some protein, she parked in front of the diner.

The bell tinkled above the door as she entered the restaurant. Her mouth watered when the smell of bacon and coffee blanketed her. A sign said to seat yourself, so she went to the back close to the window.

"Howdy. Would you like some coffee?" the waitress asked.

Jillian looked at her name tag, "I would, thank you, Sandy."

The woman flipped the cup over and poured the black gold brew. "Would you like a moment to look at the menu?"

"Yes please, thanks." Jillian said accepting the proffered menu.

Pictures of mouthwatering food filled the menu making her stomach growl. Finally, she settled just as Sandy stepped up to her table. "Are you ready?"

"Yes, I'll have a short stack with two eggs over medium, two strips of bacon, and one sausage patty." She ordered.

"I'll have it right out to you." Sandy left her to sip her coffee.

Peace settled over her as she watched two old men playing checkers two tables over. A tall Native American sat with a beautiful brunette eating their breakfast. She recognized him as the person who rode with Frank to help with the twins yesterday.

Briefly she wondered how the little girls were, when Sandy place the platter in front of her. "Will there be anything else?"

"This will do thanks." Jillian smiled up at her.

Tucking into the delicious food, her attention fell on the door when it opened. Detective Wolf stepped inside to look around. When his eyes fell on her, she could tell he was on official business. Why he wanted to speak with her she had no idea.

"Miss Taylor?" he stopped at the table. "May I have a word?"

"Yes, have a seat." She answered warily.

"I've been in touch with your realtor and she confirmed you purchased the ranch." He said. "May I ask, what are your plans for the place?"

"You can ask." She replied. Something about him rubbed her wrong, despite her better judgement.

"Just curious." He replied when Sandy appeared with a cup and coffee.

"Thanks, Sandy." He smiled up at her.

"I do have a couple of questions maybe you could help me with." Jillian said watching the waitress batt her eyelashes at him.

"Shoot." He turned his attention back to her.

"Where would I find a car dealership and a furniture store?" she asked.

"You'll have to drive to Sheridan for those kind of stores." He replied thoughtfully.

"And what direction would that be from here?" she asked.

"East, you know I could take you if that's something you'd want." He offered.

Jillian chewed the bacon she had just placed in her mouth. "Don't you have to work?"

"Yes. It just so happens I have business in Sheridan today." He said.

"In that case, I would welcome the company." She agreed. "I don't know anything about trading a car in for a truck, and I'm going to purchase a few pieces of furniture while I'm there."

"I'll go let my boss know it will be late when I return." He stood to his feet.

"I'll meet you out front when I'm done" she smiled.

Jillian finished the savory meal enjoying every bite. It occurred to her she hadn't eaten since she'd arrived at the ranch. So many things happened, by the time she had everything all cleaned up, she dropped onto the pallet she'd made in complete exhaustion.

She paid for her meal and hurried outside to her car.

Josh met her on the sidewalk and they walked to city hall to get her utilities turned on. When they returned to the car she allowed him to drive since she had no idea where she was going.

The drive to Sheridan was a long one. Josh peppered her with questions she refused to answer. It bothered her that some of those questions were suspicious. Did he think she was a criminal? She just arrived in Wolf Creek and felt as though he intended to find something to arrest her for.

"Josh?" she interrupted him. "Do you think I'm some kind of felon on the run? I've done nothing illegal in my entire life. Shoot I don't even have a parking ticket on my record."

"Sorry." He felt bad for making her feel that way. "I just became a detective last week. I'm a bit too enthusiastic."

"Rest assured I'll not break any laws in your town." She said as Sheridan appeared on the horizon.

The truck dealership was an experience she never wanted to go through again. On this occasion, she was grateful for Josh's experience.

"Jillian," he whispered. "Your car is worth more than what he's offering, and that truck, although it's three years old isn't worth what they're asking."

"What do I do?" she really liked the royal blue color.

"Let's test drive it first." He said.

The salesman rode with them around the town. When they returned he asked if she was satisfied.

"May I have a few minutes to discuss it with Josh." She asked.

"Surely, I'll just pop into my office for a moment." The man said walking away.

"What do you think Josh?" she asked uncertain of the deal.

"Will you allow me to negotiate the price for you?" he asked, "That is if this is the one you're comfortable with."

She agreed and followed him inside the dealership, shivering from the cool air that greeted them after being in the sunshine.

"What did you decide." The man asked.

"The car is worth at least three thousand more than you're offering." Josh spoke. "If you'll give her eight thousand for the car, we'll take the truck at two thousand less than the sticker price."

"Look sir. I'm giving her an awesome deal on that truck. There's only eight thousand miles on it." He disagreed. "The car has well over ninety thousand miles."

"The point is the car is in pristine shape." Josh said. "That is a used truck. You and I both know that you lose several thousand off the value when it's driven off the lot."

"Okay, here's what I'll do. Six thousand for the car and she drives the truck off the lot for one thousand less than the sticker price." He negotiated.

"Done." Josh said turning to Jillian. "Is that satisfactory?"

"Yes, thank you." She smiled at him.

She signed the paperwork and the salesman accepted the check for the balance due. She walked out of the dealership with the keys to a really nice truck.

"Are you hungry?" Josh asked, "I'm buying."

"Sure, where to?" she said starting the engine.

"The steak house we passed on the way in." he said.

After a leisurely lunch, she drove him to the police station so he could take care of his business with them. While he was inside, she went to the small furniture store and found a good deal on a bedroom set. The men loaded the set into her truck along with a kitchen table and chairs.

When she picked Josh up, they went to the big box store on the way out of town. She purchased bedding, dishes, pots, and pans before they drove to Wolf Creek.

"If you want I'll come to the ranch to help unload your furniture." He offered when she stopped at the police station to drop him off.

"Okay, I'm going to that little store to get a few things." She said. "I'll see you at the ranch."

Jillian parked in front of Brown's General Store and went inside. She thought it was a bit strange no one greeted her. Quickly taking the small basket she began filling it with fresh produce and fruit. When she went back to the front to pay, no one was around.

"Hello?" she called out but received no answer.

Remembering the door at the back of the store, she knocked before opening it to a large storeroom. To the right of the entrance another door stood open. After knocking she stepped into the doorway and the words she intended to say died on her lips.

The little old woman she assumed owned the place lay face down on the carpet.

After checking for a pulse, she called the police station.

Chapter Five

"Hi Josh." Kimberly greeted him. "Where have you been all day?"

"I had some business to attend to in Sheridan. Is Joe in?" He asked.

"Yes, he's on the phone." Kimberly said as she answered another call.

Josh went to Joe's office and gave him the paperwork he received from the police chief in Sheridan.

"Josh!" Kimberly called out. "Someone just called to report they found Mrs. Mavis dead!"

Josh rushed outside followed by Joe. Joe stopped at Doc's office on the way as Josh ran the two blocks to the General Store.

Jillian sat in a chair waiting for the police to arrive. She jumped up to meet them when she heard the bell over the door.

Josh stepped into the tiny apartment followed by Joe and Doc.

"What happened?" he asked falling into his detective role.

"When I came in, no one seemed to be around. I knocked on the door to the storage room. After waiting, I noticed the open door to the apartment and knocked. When I received no answer I stepped inside to find this lady." She explained pointing to the old woman.

Doc examined her while Josh finished asking Jillian questions, "She's been dead for at least two hours. I suspect her heart gave out on her. I've been after her to slow down, but we all know how stubborn the woman was."

Jillian sat back down shaking. What are the odds that she would find two dead women in two days?

Josh noted the color drain from her face, "Doc, uh, I think Jillian may pass out on us." He reached out to catch her as she slid out of the chair.

"She'll be okay. At any rate, take her to my office and I'll check her over." Doc said waving smelling salt under her nose.

Then he and Joe placed Mrs. Mavis in a body bag and took her to the new morgue.

Jillian was grateful that Josh helped her across the street. So much had happened to her over the last few weeks that finding the shopkeeper was the last straw.

Josh sat in the waiting room while Doc gave Jillian a checkup. He dug his cell phone out and call Trace.

"Hello?" he answered.

"Hey. It's Josh, can you meet me at the old ranch down the road from Old man McMurphy's in an hour?" Josh asked.

"Sure, what's up?" he agreed.

"A woman named Jillian Taylor bought it and she needs help moving some furniture in." Josh explained. "If you can get Will to help we can unload it in about a half hour."

"I'm sure Will won't mind. We'll be there." He said ending the call.

Doc gave Jillian a thorough examination to be sure nothing other than shock had caused her to faint.

"Well little lady, you are in good health, but you need to get some rest and eat a little more food." He said. "You're about fifteen pounds underweight."

"I know. I've had a rough few months." She sighed.

"Tell me what's going on?" he insisted.

34

"I buried my abusive husband three weeks ago and decided to move here after I found that small ranch for sale." She reluctantly unburdened herself. "Then I show up here and find that other woman dead and her twins, and now this."

"My advice is to get some good food in you and rest for a few days." He said holding up his hand to silence her protest. "I know you have your work cut out for you since the ranch has been vacant for quite some time. Just don't do too much. Here, take these vitamins and I want to see you next month."

"Okay Doctor Sims." She accepted the bottle he gave her. "Thank you."

"Just call me Doc." He smiled at her as he opened the door for her to go.

Jillian stopped at Sally's desk to pay the bill and make a follow-up appointment.

Josh opened the door for her and followed her outside. "Do you need me to drive you home?"

"No thanks, I'll be fine." She shook her head. "I didn't get to buy the stuff I needed at that little store."

"No worries. I'll call Mrs. Andrews. She helped Mrs. Mavis most of the time." He replied. "If you want to wait, I'm sure she'll come right over."

"That would be perfect." She walked with him to the store.

Fifteen minutes later Jillian was on her way home while Josh consoled Mrs. Andrews. He told her to expect his brothers to arrive.

Jillian backed the truck close to the front door as an unfamiliar truck parked by the barn. She knew immediately they were Josh's brothers since they were older versions of him.

"Hi, I'm Will Wolf." He introduced himself. "This is my brother Trace."

"It's a pleasure to meet you." She relaxed in their presence. "Josh had some business to take care of. He should be here shortly."

"No worries." Will smiled at her. "So, you're the new owner?"

"Yes I am," she responded feeling safe around the two brothers.

"Are you gonna run this place by yourself?" Trace asked surprised.

"I have a few ideas in mind after I get settled in." she answered. "I'll need to speak with the mayor or the city council about my ideas."

"You're in luck." Trace grinned. "Will is the mayor."

Jillian turned surprised eyes on Will. "This is great. Could we talk about my plans until Josh arrives to help."

"No problem, shoot." Will agreed.

"I want to set up a camp to teach children how to ride and care for horses." She said. "I would also like to help disabled children and adults utilizing the horses and special equipment as therapy."

"That's a mighty big plan." Will studied her for a moment. "I'll tell you what. Put that on paper and we'll discuss it at our next meeting Monday at six p.m."

"Do you want the financial information too?" she asked excitedly.

"Not for the first meeting. If the counsel likes the idea, we'll proceed from there." Will answered as Josh drove up.

"How is Mrs. Andrews?" Jillian asked as he approached the group.

"What's wrong with mom?" Will asked worry furrowing his brow.

"Mrs. Mavis passed away and I had to have her come close up the store." Josh broke the news.

36

The brothers mouths gaped open as what he said registered. "When? How?" Will finally asked.

"Doc said sometime around noon." Josh said. "Jillian is the one who found her."

"I'm sorry for the loss of the poor woman." She looked at each brother.

"Let's get this stuff unloaded." Josh moved to open the tailgate.

Jillian opened the door and directed them upstairs to the master bedroom where her little pallet still lay on the floor. She quickly shoved it into the corner as they put the frame together.

Next came the mattress and boxed springs they placed in the frame.

She made the bed while they brought the rest of the items in the bedroom set upstairs. When they brought the table in she showed them where she wanted it.

Weary from the long day, she waved at the two brothers when they left. Josh lit the pilot light on the hot water tank and stove, then made sure she didn't need anything else before he left. It was a blessing to have the utilities on, she thought watching the tub fill with hot water.

After adding Lilac scented bath beads, she finally sat down letting her body relax. For the first time in several years she allowed herself to grieve the many losses in her life. The dam of tears burst as she sobbed. Most of all she cried for the years she wasted with Terry.

Completely spent, she drained the water from the tub and dried off with the new fluffy towels she purchased. Slipping into her worn nightshirt, she sank into the bed and allowed sleep to claim.

Chapter Six

Josh slipped into the seat next to Joe at the back of the courtroom for the trials they had to testify in. "Have they called you yet?"

"No, the case is up next." He replied as the bailiff called "Mrs. Ethel Davis!"

Ethel stood behind the desk with the court appointed defense attorney.

"Do you understand the charges against you Ms. Davis?" Judge Odom asked.

"Yes sir." She sniffed.

"How do you plead?" he asked.

"Not guilty your Honor." Her attorney said.

"You are so guilty!" Sadie Walsh jumped to her feet waving her fist.

"Order!" he slammed his gavel on the desk. "Ms. Walsh you will refrain from another outburst or I'll hold you in contempt of court! Miss Gunn call your witness."

"Sheriff Joe Dodson." She called.

After swearing in, Joe sat in the witness stand.

"Sheriff Dodson, would you tell the court about the incident that occurred on five, twelve?"

"I answered a call to the defendant's home at oh nine hundred. When I arrived, Ms. Walsh and Ms. Davis were engaged in an intense argument." He testified. "I stepped from my vehicle when Ms. Davis assaulted Ms. Walsh with her cane. Before I could restrain them, Ms. Walsh hit Ms. Davis in the face."

"How often have you been called to the defendant's home?" Miss Gunn asked.

"Almost daily, for years." He replied.

"What were they arguing over?" she asked.

"Ms. Walsh owns a chihuahua named Brutus, who loves to chase Ms. Davis cat, Tiger, up the tree growing between their houses." He answered. "I've arrested them numerous times and confiscated the animals. Things are good for a few days then they begin the arguments all over again."

"Thank you, Sheriff Dodson." Miss Gunn said turning to the defense attorney. "Your witness."

"Sheriff are you sure Ms. Davis assaulted Ms. Walsh first and not the other way around?" he asked.

"The women live two blocks from the station. I could see everything from my jeep. Ms. Davis struck Ms. Walsh first." He said calmly.

"No further questions, your Honor." The attorney knew the case was good against the woman. She insisted she wasn't guilty, but the facts were against her.

"Ms. Davis, I sentence you to thirty days in jail, and a fifty dollar fine." Judge Odom ordered. "Ms. Walsh, you will also spend thirty days in jail, and a fifty dollar fine. Your animals will remain in custody at the county veterinarians office until you're released. Should you have to appear before my court again, I'll order the animals removed from your residence. Am I clear?"

Both women agreed crying as Joe escorted them both back to the jail.

"Next case!" Judge Odom ordered.

"Bernard, Preston, and Reginald Alexander." The bailiff called.

The boys sat down next to the high-powered attorney their parents called in from Sheridan.

"You boys have been busy." Judge Odom said after the bailiff read the charges against them. "How do you plead?"

"Not guilty your Honor." Their lawyer, Mr. O'Conner replied for them.

Josh didn't care for the man's smug attitude, but he wasn't worried. The evidence was iron clad. Especially since Will and Samantha sat in the hall waiting to testify. James was already waiting when he got there.

"Miss Gunn?" Judge Odom said. "You may proceed."

The prosecutor called every witness who testified to what they'd seen. Then she called Will Wolf to the stand. After swearing to tell the truth, he sat patiently waiting for Miss Gunn to question him.

"Mr. Wolf. Tell the court what happened on the day in question." Miss Gunn asked.

Will told the court how he had come out of the barn to find the suspect waving a shot gun at his wife and three children. Then went on to say how he'd disarmed the young man as his brother Detective Wolf rode up on his horse to take the man into custody.

"That's all the questions I have for the witness." She sat behind her little table.

"Mr. O'Conner you may cross examine the witness." The Judge said.

"Yes, your Honor." The man stood to his feet. "Mr. Wolf isn't it true that you suffer from PTSD. Did you assault a man in the woods south of town and you yourself killed the same man with your bare hands behind the Wild Mustang Bar & Grill?"

"Objection your Honor!" Miss Gunn spoke up.

"Sustained." The judge agreed. "You don't have to answer those questions Mr. Wolf."

"I want to your honor." Will said earning a shake of the prosecutor's head. "Yes I do suffer from PTSD, but in recent years I've improved immensely. As to the rest, yes I did assault and eventually killed the same man. What you didn't say

40

was the man had kidnapped, tortured, and put my now wife in a coma. Later after she recovered, that man escaped and I saved the then bar owner, Ginger Smalley-Goines from him. The Sheriff of Wolf Creek declared it was self-defense."

"Why did you retire from the Military?" he pushed.

"That, Sir, I will not answer. I had my reasons and those who need to know already have that information." Will glared at the man.

"Well, I submit that you had a flash back and tackled Mr. Preston Alexander upon seeing the rifle. I would like to add, it was empty and posed no threat to anyone." He said smugly.

"While it's true my training from the military kicked in, I didn't know the rifle to be empty." Will squared his shoulders. "My wife and three children sat on a blanket terrified by the man waving that rifle. It was and is my duty as a husband and father to protect my family no matter what."

"Are you completely sure the man posed a danger to anyone?" the man asked confident he had him.

"As a highly decorated Special Forces Lieutenant in the Military, I stand by everything I've said." Will answered.

"Isn't it true that your actions on the last mission you went on that due to your incompetence two of your teammates died and several sustained severe injuries?" the man strayed into classified information.

"If you have that information, you've broken the law. I want to know how you came to have it in your possession." Will asked glaring at the man.

"I uh, obtained a court order to retrieve those files." The man said nervously.

"What judge gave that order?" Will asked.

41

"If you don't mind sir, I'm asking the questions here. But suffice to say I have the complete record."

Will studied the man for a moment then looked at the judge. "Sir, I am unable to answer questions about classified government records."

"I will look into it." The judge nodded. "I'm ready to rule on this case."

"But your Honor…" the attorney sputtered.

"Bailiff detain this man." He ordered. After the bailiff removed the lawyer, Judge Odom turned his full attention onto the defendants. "Preston Alexander, I find you guilty of all charges. You will spend two years in jail, three years of probation after you've served your time and a ten thousand dollar fine. Bernard Alexander, guilty of all charges, your sentence is one year in prison followed by two years of probation, and a five thousand dollar fine. Reginald Alexander, guilty of all charges. One year in prison followed by two years of probation, and a five thousand dollar fine. Court adjourned"

Joe returned in time to help escort the prisoners back to the jail to await transfer to the state penitentiary. After they left the judge requested Will to meet him in his chambers.

"Mr. Wolf, how would you like to handle this situation." He asked.

"Call General Daniel Ames, he'll send MP's for the man." Will said handing him the number. "He'll get to the bottom of this."

"Thank you. I didn't really want to be on the hook for this one." Judge Odom smiled with relief.

"You're welcome." Will said turning to leave. "See you at the meeting on Monday evening."

Chapter Seven

Long fingers of sunlight crept slowly across Jillian's bed. Taking a moment she stretched as far as she could waking her tired muscles. Today was going to be a long day. Her first order of business was a giant cup of coffee and breakfast, after she dressed.

She opened the doors and windows upstairs to air out the rooms, then did the same downstairs. When she opened the kitchen door, she squeaked in surprise to find Josh with his fist raised to knock on the door.

"What are you doing here?" she asked holding her hand over her racing heart.

"I normally come by to make sure everything is okay." He said. "It's just a part of my routine."

"Would you like a cup of coffee since you're here?" she opened the screen door.

"I don't mind if I do." He smiled making her heart flutter.

He sat at the new table and watched her make the coffee. "How was your second night here?"

"It was great." She replied with a smile. "I actually got some rest for the first time in years."

"Will told me about the business you're hoping to set up and I think it's a fantastic idea." He said.

"I've always had a passion to teach others to ride, and I did some research on therapy for the disabled." She had a far off look in her eyes. "One of my niece's had a birth defect when she was born. Sadly, she died when she was seven because of it."

"I'm sorry for your loss." Josh's voice held compassion instead of pity.

"Thanks. The most wonderful experience for Myra was being in the Special Olympics. I'll always remember the look on her little face when she won an award." She explained blinking back tears.

"So, what all do you have to accomplish to get your camp ready?" Josh asked.

Grateful for the change of subject, she answered. "I need to update the barn and add a bigger corral, before finding the horses I'll need. Then purchase the saddles and special equipment for disabled riders. When the equipment arrives I'll start training the horses."

"How can I help?" he asked before he could change his mind.

"It all depends on what the City Council has to say tonight." She said surprised.

"Do you have your proposal written up yet?" he asked.

"Yes, I have the draft. I'll set my computer and printer up after breakfast and finish the final proposal." She answered.

"That's good, I should get going, I have a few more miles to cover before going back to the station." He drained the cup of coffee. "I'll see you at the meeting."

After breakfast, Jillian set up her laptop and printer on one end of the dining room table. Finished with the proposal, she went to the living room and deep cleaned it and the downstairs half bath.

Lunch came and went until she realized she needed to get ready for the meeting. A quick shower and makeup job left her with just enough time to get to the city hall.

Josh stood at the back of the room waiting for Jillian. Something about that woman spoke to the loneliness deep down inside of him. Of course he felt attracted to her, but the feeling was much more intense than any other he had ever experienced. He wouldn't tell anyone yet, at least not until he had a name to put to it.

Jillian stepped into the room and squeaked when Josh appeared at her side. "Don't do that." She put her hand over her heart.

"Sorry, I was trained by the best to walk softly." He grinned as he escorted her to a seat at the front next to Frank and Trace. Will sat in one of the chairs on the small stage.

First on the agenda, the clerk, Alma Jensen, conducted the roll call, then went on to read the minutes from the last meeting. The discussion became a little heated between the town banker, Donald Marshall, and the town realtor, Dennis Berkley, over purchasing a large plot of land just south of town for a huge multipurpose park.

"It's the perfect place for a park. Wolf Creek will provide several water activities during the summer." Dennis insisted.

"You just want to broker the deal so you can line your pockets!" Donald growled. "How much money does Mr. Foster want for the property. If I recall it's a part of his ranch."

"It's a ten-acre plot, and he's asking a fair price for it." Dennis named the number.

"How much do we have in the account Ms. Watson?" Will asked the town treasurer.

The discussion continued for five more minutes until everyone agreed to wait for the next meeting while they explored the need for the park. Dennis cautioned them the only reason Mr. Foster wanted to sell was he needed money.

"Miss Jillian Taylor has the floor for the next order of business." The clerk said.

"Go on, you can do this." Josh encouraged her.

Jillian stepped to the counsel and handed them copies of her proposal. "Um… Thanks for allowing me to speak."

Her eyes sought out Josh for his encouragement.

"I want to open a clinic to teach children to ride horses, and in the near future it will open to disabled children and adults as therapy." She continued reading the proposal to those who were in attendance.

"I don't understand, are you asking the town to foot the bill?" Donald asked.

"No sir, I have the funds to take care of it myself." She frowned at him. "I'm asking for approval to put my plan in place."

"Just where are you going to put this camp?" Dennis asked seeing dollar signs.

"I have purchased the small ranch just west of town." She replied as disappointment crossed Dennis' face.

"When are you planning to begin?" Will asked.

"The minute I get the permits." Jillian replied. "I'm also planning to hire local contractors to do the work. I'm working on the draft of the renovations to the barn and adding a larger corral with a small stadium seating area for parents to watch."

"May we have until the next meeting in a month to talk about this?" Will asked. "By then you should have the blueprints of your renovations."

"That's fair." She agreed. "Thank you for considering my proposal."

After they had a light discussion from those in attendance, the clerk ended the meeting.

Josh walked Jillian to her new truck when she finished answering questions from those interested in her idea. She also walked away with a fist full of business cards.

"I'd say you have a good chance of gaining the approval from the town counsel." Josh opened the door to her truck.

"Technically I don't need their permission since I'll be out of city or in this case town limits." She said. "However, I want to stay on the good side of the township."

"That's a smart move." He grinned. "Are you okay to drive home in the dark?"

"Yes, you silly man." She giggled. "I've been taking care of myself for a while now."

Josh shoved his hands into his pockets and said, "If you need anything you can call me."

"No I can't." she said somberly.

"Why not?" his mouth dropped open.

"I don't have your number." She laughed.

"Well I can take care of that right now." He pulled out his phone. "What's your number?"

She rattled it off and he called her cell phone. "Now you have mine too."

"Thanks for supporting me back there. You don't know how much it meant to me." She said.

"You're welcome." He replied. "Be safe going home."

With a nod of her head she backed out and drove away with him staring at the lights of her truck until they disappeared.

"Uh-oh." Trace chuckled behind him. "Looks like someone has been bitten by the love bug."

"Not yet I ain't." Josh scowled at his brother. "I am just being nice to her. She's got no family nearby."

"From what I saw just now, you're definitely smitten." Will joined in teasing him.

"Believe what you want," he said tersely. "I know how I feel and it don't matter what y'all or anyone else thinks. I'll see y'all later."

47

Josh got into his truck and headed home thinking about the gorgeous woman. Shoot they hadn't even went on a date yet and he couldn't stop thinking about her. He didn't count the trip to Sheridan as a date. He went to do some business and offered to help her.

It was a plus that she lived only a few miles away from the ranch. That way he could check on her every day. He parked in the drive and checked the locks on the barn. Then he went inside the house locking it up on his way to bed. When he slipped between the sheets, loneliness crept over him. For a long time he dreamed of having a good woman by his side. The pool of women in Wolf Creek had no one he wanted to marry, but since Jillian had arrived he couldn't stop thinking about her.

Flopping onto his back, he threw his arm over his eyes willing sleep to drive out the emotional turmoil wrapping its long fingers around his lonely heart.

Chapter Eight

Jillian awoke with a new purpose for the first time in a long while. Grateful for the money she inherited from her parents estate, the enormous trust fund her grandfather set up for her, and the generous life insurance policy on her ex-husband, she had millions of dollars at her disposal to do anything she wanted. Needless to say following her dream was at the top of the list.

Dressed in a t-shirt and cutoff shorts, she went downstairs to make a light breakfast. She hit the button on the coffee maker and heard a knock on the front door. When she opened it, a strange man stood on her porch with his hat in hand.

"May I help you?" she asked speaking through the locked storm door.

"Uh, yes. I'm looking for work and wondered if you might need a hand in running this place." He said as his steel gray eyes assessed her.

"What's your name?" she asked as her internal radar warned her of trouble.

"Damon Porter." He responded.

"Do you have any references?" she asked ready to slam the door in his face. Thankfully, she hadn't unlocked any windows or the kitchen door yet.

Without answering, he grabbed the handle of the door to yank it open.

Jillian slammed the door and slid the dead bolt into place. Fearing for her life, she ran for her cell phone. She dialed Josh's number as she ran upstairs when the sound of a window breaking reached her ears.

"Hello?" Josh answered before getting into his truck.

"Josh, somebody is breaking in." she hurried to explain as she hid under the bed in the master bedroom.

"I'm on my way. Hide and be quiet." He jumped into his truck and left dirt and gravel in his wake on his way down the driveway as he radioed the call in.

Jillian heard the man ransacking the downstairs rooms before his footsteps landed on the staircase.

"Come out, come out wherever you are!" the man taunted her. "I'll eventually find you!"

Jillian's heart raced so fast it felt as though it might explode. Fear of what the man would do if he found her before Josh arrived squeezed her chest.

He kicked open each bedroom door and searched until he came to her room. The door hit the wall when he flung it open. "I know you're in here."

Jillian held her breath while fear wrapped around her in a dark shroud as she saw the man's worn boots step into the room. Suppressing a shiver, sweat beaded on her forehead as the boots came closer to the bed.

***

Josh parked next to Jillian's truck and jumped out. He saw the broken window and hurried to enter the house. Once inside he heard a door upstairs hit the wall and the man shout at Jillian to come out of her hiding place.

He drew his firearm and moved like Shadow had trained him, as he cautiously hurried upstairs. The intruder stepped into the master bedroom when Josh cautiously crept onto the stair landing. Stealthily advancing on the room, he stepped inside and yelled, "Freeze!"

The man whirled around and hit him with a knife to his shoulder, then jumped him before he

50

could shoot him. As the two wrestled on the floor, Jillian slipped out of her hiding place and grabbed Josh's gun and shot the man.

Josh felt the man go limp and shoved him off onto the floor just as Joe and James showed up in the room. The siren of the ambulance grew louder as it drove up the driveway.

"Jillian? Are you okay?" he asked ignoring the blood that trickled down his arm.

"You're hurt!" she rushed to grab a towel to apply pressure on his shoulder.

Joe and James rushed to restrain the man when he started to wake up.

"I'm glad you were here to help Josh." Joe said as the paramedic's hurried to take care of both men. "James, go with them to the hospital. I'll question Jillian then meet you there.

Jillian sat on the porch swing as James drove away. Joe sat on the chair near the swing.

"What happened?" he asked.

She shivered while explaining the entire incident.

"Had you ever met the man before?" he asked.

"No, he said his name was Damon Porter and grabbed the door handle." she shook her head.

"That's all for now." He said getting to his feet, "I'll take you to the hospital so Doc can check you over."

"No need, I'm fine. Just a little scared is all." She declined. "But I do want to go to the hospital and check on Josh."

"I'll follow you in." he insisted.

Jillian grabbed her purse and keys, then led the way to the hospital. Joe appeared at her door to open it before she shut the engine down.

"Thank you sheriff." She smiled at him.

"You're welcome." Joe said and walked with her inside noting the Wolf family sitting in the waiting room. "You are welcome to sit with the family if you'd like."

"Thanks again." She took a seat in the small area.

"What happened Joe?" Will asked.

"Jillian can tell you better than I can." Joe replied. "I'm gonna go check on Josh."

Will turned to Jillian with questions that needed answers. Samantha knew that look and intervened. "Jillian, can you tell us what happened?"

She told them everything as the shock began to wear off. Tears fell unchecked from her eyes and she began to tremble.

"It's over now." Samantha hugged her. "Your safe."

"Thank you for shooting the man." Will managed.

"I... shot a man..." the realization of what she had done hit her.

"You saved Josh's life, if you hadn't shot him Josh might have died." Trace's voice cracked.

Doc Sims chose that moment to step into the waiting room. "He's going to survive. In fact they're releasing him now. He had ten stitches and lost a little blood."

"That's good news!" Will relaxed.

"How are you Miss Taylor?" Doc noticed the pallor of her skin.

"She just realized she shot someone." Samantha said.

"I'll be okay," she managed.

"If you need anything Miss Taylor, just call." Doc said. "I'm going back to work. Y'all take care, okay?"

"We will Doc." Will replied as Josh appeared.

Josh didn't talk to anyone as he zeroed in on Jillian. "Thank you." He said pulling her into a hug.

Something inside her snapped into place when she laid her head on his shoulder. "Are you in pain?"

"Nah. I suspect I might have some after the local anesthetic wears off." He replied. "We need to address the issue of you being alone out there on the ranch. That man could have killed you."

"I'll be fine." She shook her head. "I'm sure this was a one-time occurrence."

"You'd be surprised." Samantha said. "Josh is right, you need someone out there to help protect you."

"I haven't had time to hire a ranch hand yet." She replied.

"I'm calling Frank. He owns a security company and you'll need a guard when you open the ranch anyhow." Will said.

"Do you have one of his cards?" Jillian asked.

"Better yet, I'll call him now. If you want we can go by his house." Will said pulling his cellphone from his pocket.

"Okay. Someone will have to go to my house to retrieve Josh's truck. I don't think he's in any condition to drive." She agreed.

Will stepped outside to talk with Frank as Josh sat down. He insisted they use a local on him to stitch the deep wound. The pain medication was beginning to wear off.

"Frank said he'd meet us at his house." Will said.

Trace took Star home for some rest. Her due date was a month away and the summer heat took a huge toll on her. Samantha went to her mother's to pick up her children on her way home.

Will rode with Jillian and Josh to Frank's. They parked in the drive as Frank stepped from the SUV.

"Hey y'all." He waited until they were out of the truck.

"Hey Bear." Will clapped him on the shoulder.

"Let's go inside out of this heat." Frank led them onto the porch.

Ginger looked up from feeding Angela, one of the twin girls. "This is a nice surprise!" she grinned.

"Those little girls are growing like weeds!" Jillian exclaimed.

"Would you like to feed Amanda?" Ginger asked burping Angela.

"Could I?" Jillian asked hopefully.

"While you are doing that, let me ask what kind of security you are asking for?" Frank handed Amanda to her.

"I guess I need round the clock security." She said as the child latched onto the bottle.

"My feeling is she needs someone to stay twenty-four seven." Josh spoke up.

Will explained what happened at her house while Jillian cooed at the little girl looking up at her.

"I have a suggestion. Kevin is looking for something other than odd jobs now that Kimberly is pregnant." Frank said.

"I have a master suite downstairs and a huge guest room upstairs. They can have their pick of rooms. If that's an option they would consider." She said burping the little one.

"Let me talk to them and I'll get back with you. For now, I'll send Shadow out to stay until we can resolve the issue." Frank said.

"How much will you charge?" She asked.

Frank rattled off a price and she agreed. "I'll discuss Kevin's salary with him if he decides to take the job."

Chapter Nine

Kevin and Kimberly arrived a few days later to discuss working for Jillian. Shadow had left earlier in the day for a case that required the entire team.

Jillian showed them the available rooms to choose from after he accepted the job.

"I think we'll take the downstairs room since Kimmy is pregnant." Kevin said looking at his wife for confirmation.

"I'm good with that." Kimberly nodded with a smile.

"It makes sense. It's ready for you to move into. My room is upstairs at the end of the hall." Jillian agreed.

"Thank you for considering me. I'm tired of hustling odd jobs to support my growing family." Kevin said gratefully.

"After what happened the other day I'm happy you accepted the job." Jillian replied then continued the tour. "You may use the kitchen at any time. I'm a light snacker so feel free to eat whatever you want."

"Thank you for all this." Kimberly said sniffing. "Danged hormones. I had planned to live in the house where our parents left me and Kelly, but while I was away at college, Kelly and I decided to rent it out. Now I don't want to kick the tenants out."

"Well, since I'll need security when we get the camp opened, how would you feel about adding a home for you big enough you can grow into it?" Jillian asked then laid out the plans she was working on.

"That sounds great." Kimberly smiled looking around at the beautiful kitchen.

"We could build it closer to the entrance of the ranch. It would be prudent to widen the driveway to make an entrance and exit with a guard shack between them. That way we can control who has access to the ranch. Automatic gates would be helpful as well." Kevin suggested. "Frank will set up cameras for us so that his team can monitor remotely while I can see everything from the guard shack."

"It would take them close to three hours to get here from Sheridan." She said.

"Frank has so much business from Wolf Creek now, he's opening a remote office on the ground floor of the house he owns in town." Kevin explained. "He'll still use it for a safe house until he can find another one. The guys who work the bar security sleep there too."

Jillian opened her mouth to say something when her phone buzzed for the millionth time. Her family had been calling nonstop. She could let it go to voicemail, but her box was full. "Excuse me, I need to take this." She apologized and stepped outside. "Hello Carol."

"Well it's about time you answered your phone! Do you know how worried we've been?" her sister hissed. "Jeb is ready to call out the national guard to track you down."

"I'm sorry, but if you knew of my plans, y'all would've talked me out of it. Now that you know I'm okay, you can tell the others." She said.

"Oh no you don't! I ain't telling Jeb anything. You have no idea what I've been putting up with since you left. Although I'm relieved you're okay, I'm a bit angry with you." Carol retorted.

"I know, and I'm sorry. I just wish everyone would stop nagging me and let me live my life the way I want to. Between Jeb wanting to invest and control my money, and Lucy already trying to fix me up with her high-class friends, I can't take any more." She apologized.

"I get it sis, but you could've at least let one of us know you were leaving." Carol sighed. "I was worried sick."

"I'm fine. In fact, between our inheritance, my trust fund, and Terry's large life insurance policy, I'm fulfilling my dream. I found a small ranch and bought it." She told her sister enthusiastically.

"So you're really going to do it? Can you at least tell me where you are?" Carol asked in a resigned voice.

"If you can keep from telling Jeb and Lucy. I'll call Cal later this evening." She insisted.

"You know keeping our brother and sister in the dark is going to make it harder on you in the long run." Carol warned her. "I wouldn't want to be around when you do call them."

"I need to go Carol. My friend is here and I need to talk to him." She told her.

"As in boyfriend?" Carol sounded hopeful.

"It's too soon for that. Good grief, Terry's barely been in the ground for a month yet and y'all are already trying to get me hooked up with someone." Jillian moaned. "I'll talk to you later."

Jillian ended the call on the protest of her sister. She loved her family dearly but there were times they drove her crazy. Thankfully, Carol and Cal usually gave her space when she needed it. Jeb and Lucy on the other hand were overbearing and thought everyone should take their advice on everything. It got worse when their parents passed away.

Josh parked next to Kevin's truck happy he had accepted the job from Jillian. He could breathe a bit easier knowing he was there to protect her.

His breath caught when Jillian stepped off the porch to meet him.

"Hi Josh." She said nervously. The woodsy smell that was all Josh, drifted on the slight breeze to wrap itself around her.

"Hey. How are things?" he asked.

"Good." She simply replied.

"What's wrong Jilly?" he asked.

"Nothing really. I just got off the phone with my sister. The family isn't too happy because I didn't consult them before leaving." She shrugged.

"Family can be taxing sometimes. So Kevin and Kimberly are going to move in here with you?" he asked.

"Yes, they are. Come on in for some tea." She suggested moving toward the door.

"Thanks." He bowed to let her lead the way.

They went inside where Kevin and Kimberly were sitting at the table looking over the rough draft of her plans.

"I'll get the tea, so have a seat." Jillian said stepping into the kitchen.

"Hey Josh, how's the shoulder?" Kevin greeted him.

"Good as new. I was lucky that Jillian was here." He said with pride in his eyes as he watched her pour tea into glasses.

Kevin noticed the longing in Josh and Jillian's eyes when they thought no one was looking but he remained silent.

"Are those the plans for your camp?" Josh asked Jillian when she place the tea in front of him.

"Yes. Kevin has some great suggestions like putting a guard shack between a lane for entering the ranch on one side and exiting on the other side. It would give us control over who comes and goes." She said. "In fact, he's going to head up the overall security of the ranch."

"Eventually we'll have to employ a few more guards to patrol the area and rotate shifts. For now I can handle everything since I'm staying in the house." Kevin spoke up.

Josh and Kevin continued their discussion while Kimberly and Jillian pulled together a simple but filling meal.

They enjoyed a leisurely visit until Josh decided to go home. Jillian walked him out while Kevin and Kimberly retired for the evening.

"I enjoyed your visit." Jillian stopped on the porch.

"It was fun. I love the plans you have for the camp, and I'd love to be a part of it." Josh said.

"I'm sure we could find something for you to do." She grinned. "I mean look at this place. It's not falling down, but it sure needs a face lift. The other buildings we want to build are just in the idea stage."

Enchanted by her enthusiasm, Josh couldn't help himself. Much to her surprise he brushed her lips with his. Normally she would have pushed him away but found she was too weak to move.

Josh stepped back and rubbed the back of his neck. "I uh… I should go."

"Okay." She managed in a normal voice.

He reached out and pushed a lock of hair behind her ear then cupped her cheek. "I'll come see you tomorrow."

Closing her eyes she could only nod her head. Then he left her standing on the porch feeling too many emotions to count. With one final wave, she watched the taillights of his truck fade in the distance.

She sank onto the porch swing with her fingers touching her lips. This feeling came from a place so deep in her heart she had no idea what it was. None of the few boyfriends she had, including her deceased husband made her feel so special.

Finally realizing how late it was, she made her way inside to go to bed. Kevin met her coming from locking the back door and windows.

"Good night, Ms. Taylor." He said with a knowing smile.

"Please call me Jillian. You and Kimberly are living here now. There's no need to be so formal." She blushed. "Good night Kevin."

"As you wish Jillian." He bowed as she passed him to go upstairs to her room.

Even after the long shower she took, processing what had just happened kept her awake long into the night.

***

Josh slipped between the sheets of his bed still thinking about Jillian. It was a mistake to kiss her since he still didn't know much about her, but he couldn't help himself. The lady intrigued him and when he kissed her every emotion he'd ever had didn't compare to the feelings that speared his heart.

With a snort, he rolled over. He could hear it now from his brothers, *It's about time the love bug hit you." Trace's voice ran through his head. Will's voice followed, "I knew you'd get bit one of these days."*

Forcing himself to forget everything, he tried to get some sleep. Tomorrow was a long day with court and running down leads on the twin girls. So far everything he turned up with was dead ends. If nothing popped tomorrow, he'd recommend to Joe that the babies go into foster care or adoption.

Chapter Ten

Josh went through the responses he'd received from the inquiries about Jolinda Gray. The information proved his hunch was right in that someone filed a stolen car report on the Plymouth she drove dated eight months prior in Austin, Texas. He had already determined her driver's license was fake. The most disturbing item was the real Jolinda Gray died twenty years ago. With no more leads he found himself hitting the proverbial brick wall.

"Come in Josh, what's on your mind?" Joe looked up from his computer happy for a break.

"After three months of searching for information on Jolinda Gray, all I've come up with is a stolen identity and car." He handed the file to his boss.

"Then we need to go see Miss Gunn." Joe said standing to his feet. "Let's go."

Josh followed as they went to city hall to speak with the District Attorney. Deep down he hoped she would recommend Frank and Ginger to just adopt the girls. The twins were healthy and well-adjusted from what he could tell. If the authorities took them away, Ginger would be devastated and honestly so would Frank even though he might not show it.

Miss Gunn looked up from a folder she was reading when her secretary ushered them into her office. "What can I do for you gentlemen?"

Josh handed her the file and sat down waiting for Joe to speak.

"Josh why don't you give her the facts about the case." Joe said.

Miss Gunn turned her attention to Josh waiting patiently for him to speak.

"I did an extensive search for Jolinda Gray and found she died twenty years ago and there was a stolen car report on the car that she drove and wrecked. I've checked both state and federal databases for her identity using fingerprints but found nothing. " Josh explained. "The twin girls we found next to their deceased mother are in the care of Frank and Ginger Goines."

"How are the babies?" she asked.

"Thriving. They are well adjusted and in good health." Josh replied. "I would like to suggest that the girls be left in the custody of the Goines."

"I'll have to do some research on the family before we can make anything permanent." She said.

Joe spoke up, "I can assure you they are good people. Frank owns Charlie Foxtrot Security Inc, which is one of the top security agencies in several states. Ginger, while she had some difficulties before marrying Frank, has become one of the best mother's in the area."

"What kind of difficulties?" she asked.

"Well, she lost her parents when she was a teenager and helped her two older brothers to raise the three younger ones, two of which were four-year-old twins and helped keep their large ranch running. Those around her often teased or left her out of the activities most kids enjoyed. The only female presence in her life was Josh's mother."

"I'll look into everything and get back with you. For now the twins may stay where they are." She said. "If there's nothing else, I have to be in court in about five minutes."

"No problem. Let us know if there are any questions or concerns you have." Joe stood to leave.

Josh wanted to tell Frank and Ginger what was going on, but it would be unethical for him to disclose information.

"Have you seen Miss Taylor since the break in?" Joe asked.

"Yes, Kevin and Kimberly have moved into the house with her. Kevin is her new security guard." Josh replied. "You should see the plans they're working on. It's gonna be awesome for the people she's catering to."

"I'd like to know where she got all that money." he wondered.

"All I know is she left Arkansas without telling her family and moved here." Josh shrugged.

"I'm setting James up to drive by occasionally to be sure they're ok. I feel much better knowing Kevin is there. I hate that Kimberly decided to quit though." Joe frowned.

"She wants to enjoy her pregnancy instead of having to work. Since Kevin is the security guard, he's making twice the money she did." Josh said.

"Now we gotta find someone to fill her spot." Joe shrugged.

"How about her sister Kelly?" Josh suggested. "I know she's tired of working at the bar."

"I'll give her a call. I hope she'll accept the job if she doesn't, we'll have to put an ad in the paper." Joe replied.

"I'm sure she will." Josh insisted. "Do you think Miss Gunn will allow Frank and Ginger to adopt the babies?"

"They have a good shot at it. The only problem might be Ginger's record. I know she only fought back against men who got handsy with her." Joe replied honestly.

"You know they've named the girls. To be honest at this point, everyone in that little family has bonded with them." Josh informed him.

"In the long run if they've bonded it will be a good thing. It's all up to the courts now." Joe shrugged as he opened the door to the station.

"Anything going on James?" Joe asked.

"No." he muttered.

"I get it. But someone has to fill in until we hire another dispatcher/secretary." Joe tried to ease his feelings.

"I'll take over for the afternoon." Josh offered. "You need to drive by the Taylor ranch on your rounds."

"Thanks man! I owe you." James jumped to his feet when Joe nodded his agreement.

After James left, Joe called Kelly Smalley. It still made him feel old that all the youngsters he watched over as they grew up were getting married and having children. Once again he thought about retiring.

"Hello?" Kelly answered the phone.

"Kelly? This is Joe." He said.

"Hi Joe. Do you need to talk to Brock?" she asked.

"Actually, I'd like to offer you Kimberly's position." He explained. "Since she quit, I need someone to fill the spot so my deputies can be out patrolling the area."

"Can I talk to Brock and get back to you?" she asked.

"Sure." Joe agreed then gave her the hours and rate of pay before ending the call.

Feeling a bit restless, Joe told Josh he was leaving for the rest of the day. When he got home, he grabbed his fishing pole and tackle box, then drove toward Widow's Bend. Archer retired after

Melody's funeral, and now the man had nothing to do but look at his four walls all day.

During the long drive, he thought about asking him to move to Wolf Creek. He would make a great security guard for Jillian. Since he knew Kevin, it might be the thing to get him out of mourning for the woman he loved. Anger still simmered in his heart that Falcon, the man after Star Wolf, had tortured his friend and the lady that owned the diner.

He parked in front of his friend's house to find him sitting on his porch swing staring off into the distance.

"Hey Archer!" Joe called as he got out of his jeep.

"Hey Joe, what's going on?" he waved, happy to see his longtime friend.

"I took the afternoon off. Do you wanna go fishing?" Joe asked.

"Let me get my pole and tackle box." Archer perked up a bit.

"Great." Joe watched as he went into his house.

An hour later they were sitting at their favorite spot with their lines in the water. Joe wanted to talk but decided to let Archer take the lead. In all the years they'd known each other, Joe knew his friend would open up in his own time.

"You know, I've been thinking over what you said about moving and I'm gonna do it. It's hard to let go when everything reminds me of her." He said.

"I have another idea to go along with that." Joe told him about Jillian and the business she was opening."

"That sounds like a great fit for me." He said mulling things over. "Do you think she'll hire me?"

"Maybe. You could help with the renovations until they open." Joe said happily. "Until then you can stay with me. I have that big old house with four bedrooms. There's plenty of space for you too."

"I believe I will. Thanks old friend." Archer said.

"Who are you calling old?" Joe snorted.

"If the shoe fits…" he grinned slowly coming back from his sorrow.

The friends fished for around three hours and headed back to Widow's Bend. Joe parked in front of Archer's house. "I'll help you move if you'll tell me when you're ready."

"How about next weekend. It'll give me time to pack up and put the place up for sale." He said.

"Will do. See you then." Joe waved as he drove off.

Archer waved and went inside anxious to start packing. He had a lot of stuff to get rid of and it was time.

Chapter Eleven

Jillian slowly stretched her muscles while lying in bed early on Saturday morning. Every muscle in her body hurt, but with the progress she made with those helping her proved to be well worth the pain. The last few weeks, they updated the house and made repairs, then they cleared out the barn to assess its condition.

Today she and Kevin were mapping out the cement walkways and the stalls for the rubber mats they had on order, and footings for the bunk house.

Kimberly grew bored with taking it easy as her husband insisted, so she decided to clean the house and make lunch. After which she would talk to Jillian about researching the equipment she would need for her new venture.

She placed the last platter of meat and cheese on the bar between the kitchen and dining room with a platter of vegetables, bread, condiments, plates, and silverware. The table held tea and napkins.

Kevin opened the door for Jillian following her inside.

"That looks great!" Jillian's face heated when her stomach growled loudly.

They were all nervous as they sat to eat. It was awkward living with someone you know, and even worse with someone you don't really know at all. Jillian realized Kevin and Kimberly were still essentially newlyweds. Kimberly was now beginning to show with a cute baby bump.

"Kimberly, keep track of the hours you work and I'll pay you for cooking and cleaning." She insisted.

"You don't have to do that." Kimberly shook her head.

"I insist, you can't work for free." She disagreed.

"If you really want to pay me okay." Kimberly didn't want an argument.

"I've been thinking, how do you like this house?" she asked.

"I love it." Kimberly's eyes lit up with excitement.

"Would you like to keep this one instead of building one closer to the entrance?" she asked.

"Truthfully, I'd rather keep this one. I don't want to be too close to the main road." Kimberly answered. "Plus, with the baby I don't want to move after I have it."

"Are you okay with that Kevin?" she asked.

"Yes, we can always build a tiny home for another guard later." Kevin said thoughtfully.

"That's a great idea." She made a note of it. "I'm going to start looking for a spot further back from the road for my house. I've already figured out what I want so it's just a matter of where."

"There's no hurry, so take your time. The other renovations are going as planned." Kevin said.

"I'll start looking tomorrow when the construction crew pours the flooring in the barn." She told them.

Kimberly smiled at her and said, "Maybe Josh will be free to ride with you tomorrow?"

Jillian's face heated as she ducked her head. "I wouldn't want to bother him."

"You know you want to ask him." Kimberly grinned.

"That's okay. I'll enjoy exploring my ranch alone." She shook her head.

"Do you know how to shoot a rifle?" Kevin asked.

"Yes, but it's been a long time since I've even held one." She replied.

"It would be prudent for you to take one with you. There are bears and mountain lions not to mention coyotes and wolves. I have one you can borrow until you can buy one for yourself." He insisted.

"Thanks, I'll make sure to take it with me." She agreed. "For now, I'm heading up to bed. It's been a long day. Goodnight."

The next day at breakfast, Jillian talked to Kimberly about her duties. "I'll feel much better if you don't overdo and tire yourself out too much."

"No worries. I have a husband who will push the issue." Kimberly laughed when he frowned at her. "I would also like to research some of the equipment for the campers when the time arrives to buy what you need. It would be helpful to know what kind of disabled children you're going to cater to."

"You know, I really haven't thought about that. "I guess that's something I'll need to know before we open." Jillian's face heated.

"You'll also need to have a medical building outfitted with equipment and a doctor with a nurse on staff. "The insurance protecting you from lawsuits is going to cost a chunk of money as well." Kimberly pointed out.

"I should call my brother before I go any further. "I hoped I could do this without his help." Jillian frowned.

"You seem reluctant to call him." Kevin observed.

"I love my brother dearly, but he tends to be overbearing and controlling. I'm afraid if I call him he'll either talk me out of it or insist I return to Arkansas with him." Jillian shrugged.

"Why don't you talk with a financial advisor?" Kimberly asked.

"That's what my brother is. If there was someone local, I'd be more than happy to listen." She replied.

"Let me talk to Frank. I'm sure he has someone in his vast network of clients he trusts. It can't hurt to ask." Kevin offered.

"I'll wait until you've talked to him, and I agree he is trustworthy." She smiled with relief.

"I'm going to work on dismantling the stalls in the barn." Kevin bent to kiss his wife's cheek.

"I guess it's back to work outside." Jillian said.

***

Josh crawled out of his truck tired from the day's activities. Just before he opened the back door, Trace's truck skidded to a stop beside the deck. "Hey! Star's in labor! I'm taking her to the hospital!"

Josh had no time to respond when Trace sprayed gravel and dirt driving away. He got in his truck to drive to Trace's house on the new driveway from the entrance of the ranch. After checking to be sure Trace had locked everything up and his horses fed and watered, he drove to the hospital.

He parked just as Will and Samantha got out of their SUV. Meeting them at the door, he hugged Samantha and shook his brother's hand. "I wonder how long she's going to be in labor?"

"Nobody knows, but it's a special birth since Star will have the distinction of being the first mother to deliver her baby in the new hospital." Samantha said going inside.

They met Trace at the nurses station. "I'm going to get scrubbed so I can be with her."

"You'll do fine." Samantha kissed his cheek affectionately.

"We'll be here waiting for you." Will said as the nurse asked him to follow her.

Shadow showed up just as Trace disappeared behind the doors to the labor and delivery department.

Four hours later, the Wolf family gathered around Trace at the nursery window. They watched the nurse clean Allen *Ohanzee* Wolf and wrap him in a blue blanket. She put him in a crib and rolled it to the window so everyone could see the newest member of the Wolf family.

Shadow seemed pleased when Trace told the family the baby's name.

"When can we see Star?" he asked.

"They should be finished settling her in the room." Trace said as everyone followed him down the hall.

Star looked up as the door opened and said hello with a huge smile. She had just asked for them to bring her son back to her.

"Hello my sister." Shadow spoke in their native tongue. "You have done well bringing a strong son to your husband."

"Thank you my brother." she replied with unshed tears in her eyes.

"How are you feeling Star?" Trace asked sitting next to her and holding her hand.

"I'm fine my husband." She said.

"Y'all should have seen her. I've never been so proud in my life." Trace told them. "And boy does little Allen have a set of lungs on him!"

Will put his arm around Samantha gazing at her with the same look Trace shared with Star. Something speared Josh's heart leaving an ache he couldn't describe.

"Now that I see you're okay, I'll head back home." Josh bent down to kiss Star's cheek. "Don't let Twinkle Toes boss you around sister."

71

"I won't." She giggled as Trace shot him an icy glare.

Josh left the room unable to handle the silly looks on his brother's faces. *Would he ever have that kind of love in his life?* His mind went back over the years as he counted the times he had stood with his friends as they married the loves of their lives. Some of the wives he'd hoped to court. When he finally asked the women out, they were already in a relationship.

What really bothered him were the ones who'd divorced or lost their husbands eventually came around hoping to garner his attention. He couldn't help feeling if they didn't want him back then, he didn't want to be their second choice.

He realized after Trace got married, he only went to work and home barely going out for a good time. Shoot even the Smalley twins had girlfriends, and Kelly married Brock. He passed Kevin and Kimberly so absorbed in each other they didn't even notice he passed them by.

He wondered if he was immune to whatever was in the water creating these happy couples. When he got to his truck, he slipped inside and started the engine dreading going home to that big empty house. Even though he grew up there, at times it didn't feel like home.

Parking in the drive he went to the barn to check his horses Snowball and Boots. Their soft nicker when he stepped inside the barn eased some of the emotional turmoil in his heart. He rubbed their soft velvety noses before checking their water and feed.

"I'm glad you two are here for me to talk to. I think I'd go crazy if you weren't." he sighed before locking everything up and going inside.

The house, shrouded in darkness, reminded him of a mausoleum. The thought of a snack came and went as he went upstairs to bed. Just before he drifted off, he prayed, *"Dear Lord, I know you have someone out there for me. Please keep her safe and bring her to me soon. Amen."*

He closed his eyes and allowed sleep to overtake him.

Chapter Twelve

Jillian's eyes popped open when something awakened her in the middle of the night. She laid quietly listening while staring into the darkness. There, she heard it again and relaxed. It was Kevin and Kimberly returning from the hospital. Feeling secure she rolled to her side and drifted back to sleep. Tomorrow was soon enough to find out the good news.

The next morning Kimberly told her about the new arrival the night before. After breakfast, she saddled her horse and went for a ride.

A cool breeze blew across the meadow filled with wildflowers of every color of the rainbow. The sun warmed her skin as she lifted her face to catch its golden rays while sitting on Rosebud, one of the horses she'd bought from Artie Billings.

Even though her heart was content she knew something was still missing. Terry hadn't filled the spot reserved for the love of her life. Oh she thought he was until he wasn't. She would be forever grateful that she hadn't told him of her wealth. If she had there would be no money in her accounts.

She allowed herself a few moments to draw the energizing peace from her new ranch. Rosebud shifted bringing her back from her musings. "Okay girl, let's go."

From the distance, she saw Kevin overseeing the cement workers building the frames before pouring. She turned the docile horse toward the pasture where the three horses she'd bought were grazing. After taking off her saddle and grooming her, she turned the animal loose in the same field.

Kevin looked up when she approached, "They're almost ready to pour the cement for the barn.

It was obvious that the men were unaccustomed to having a woman supervise them, so she left Kevin in charge. "I'm going inside to settle on the spot for my house."

. Kimberly loves the house and has a few ideas for decorating it." Kevin responded.

"I'm glad I made the right decision." Jillian smiled in relief leaving him to continue watching the men.

She sat down at the dining room table to look at the map of the ranch the real estate agent provided. The driveway from the entrance was almost six hundred fifty feet to the house from the main road. If she extended the drive to one of the areas she considered for her new home, it would be four times that length. The house plan she settled on came with two bedrooms, a large dining room/kitchen with the latest equipment, a spacious living room with a fireplace and floor to ceiling windows on each side, plus she could add on extra rooms later if needed. The thing that sold her was the large office with floor to ceiling bookcases and windows.

As she was deciding where to put the tiny home and the small medical building her cell phone buzzed. When she looked at the screen, a deep sigh slipped from her lips. It was time to talk to Jeb.

"Hello, Jeb." She answered.

"Where are you?" he growled. "Do you know how worried we've been?"

"Well, since I'm talking to you, it would appear that I'm just fine." She answered sarcastically. "I'm in Wolf Creek, Wyoming. And before you start making plans to come drag me back home don't."

"You need to be here with family." He insisted. "What if you need one of us and we can't be there to help?"

"I have made friends with my neighbors and they've already helped me when I needed it." Besides, I've bought a ranch and I'm going to follow my dream." She said.

"You should let me invest your money instead of wasting it on some silly dream you have." His voice rose. "If you'd let me invest your money, I promise I can double maybe even triple it."

"Jeb, that's enough. I ain't letting you anywhere near my money. I have more than enough to live my dreams. I don't need you handling any of it. I love you, but you gotta let me live my life the way I want to. She hissed.

"You don't have any idea of what you're doing!" he yelled. "You'll be broke before the year is out."

"If I am, that's my choice. I'm hanging up now." She said angrily.

She ended the call before he could respond. In need of a way to get rid of the anger she had, Jillian went for a walk to see the physical areas she would choose for her house. Between the house she lived in and the meadow she favored the most was an incline just enough to hide the field of wildflowers. The back side of the meadow featured a creek with trees lining the banks.

Her breath caught when she spotted several deer grazing near the creek. The buck with a huge rack of horns lifted his head to sniff the air. With a swish of his tail he bounded across the creek into the woods with all the other deer following.

Jillian took a deep breath allowing the peace and soft scents of the flowers to ease her tension away. Somehow she knew this was where she was supposed to be. Let her brother and sister rage all they wanted. Peace filled her heart the minute she saw the ranch. Carol and Cal would support her decision even if Jeb and Lucy didn't.

Being the middle child of the family, she usually wound up in the middle when her family had a disagreement. In her position it wasn't easy to remain neutral, but she was grateful it prepared her for life's difficulties. One huge mistake was marrying Terry, and she realized she was able to take his abuse because of her strong will. Now it was a part of her past and she would leave it there. Unfortunately, Jeb and Lucy would try to remind her of the error she'd made when they found a crack in her armor.

A huge sigh of relief slipped from her when she finally relaxed enough to make her decision before going back to the house. Jillian froze as she turned toward her home when she spotted a skunk with three babies following close behind. Sweat formed on her brow as the cute stinky animal continued toward her. She held her breath hoping it wouldn't notice her. After the little family passed by without sensing her, she turned and raced up the small hill putting as much distance as she could between them.

Kevin looked up to see Jillian running toward the house. Sensing something was wrong, he jogged to meet her.

"What's wrong Jillian?" he asked when she stopped.

"I had a run in with a skunk." She panted in relief.

Kevin managed to suppress the laughter bubbling inside. "Well, I'd say you're lucky it didn't spray you."

"I'm going inside to calm down, how close are they to being done?" she looked toward the barn.

"They're smoothing it down now. I'd say another hour before they're finished." He said.

Jillian went inside to get a cold bottle of water and sat down at the computer to look at her house plans again. While she found several she could live with, she wasn't completely satisfied with any of them. On a whim, she downloaded a program to draft her own house plan from the top three plans that caught her attention.

Several hours later, she could smell rolls and pot roast cooking. She had missed lunch since her focus remained on tweaking her house plan.

"Jillian?" Kimberly appeared in the doorway. "Dinner is ready if you are."

"I'll be right there!" she said saving the progress she made. "It smells heavenly."

They had a wonderful meal with good conversation as they got to know each other. Kevin had them in stitches telling them about some of the stunts Hawk and Shadow had pulled on him while growing up on the reservation. Jillian's cell phone rang as she finished helping Kimberly clean up. "I need to take this."

Chapter Thirteen

Josh stepped into his office to go over his reports for the many minor incidents about town. Although he wanted a big case to investigate, he was thankful there hadn't been a big crime lately. Even the two old ladies feuding over their cat and dog had been quiet since the judge fined them and gave them jail time. To be honest he missed having to go get the cat down from the tree.

Joe stuck his head in the door and told him he was taking Archer out to Jillian's. Last week he had filled in for Joe while he helped Archer move into his big house. Josh had sympathy for Archer because Falcon tortured him and the diner's owner in Widow's Bend. it took a heavy toll on the man. Especially after Melody committed suicide over it. Archer loved her so much he bought a ring to propose the day before the attack.

His phone rang bringing his focus back to his job. "Wolf."

"Josh, Larry Smalley started to open the back door to the bar and found someone had jimmied the lock. He doesn't want to go in unless you take a look first." Kelly said.

"Tell him I'm on my way. Radio James and have him meet me there." He said ending the call.

He hurried across the street as James parked his truck. They found Larry pacing at the back of the bar. "I didn't bother to open the door when I saw it was damaged." He said.

"Stay here while we go check it out." Josh ordered.

Larry watched his brother, James, and Josh slip inside without a sound, then resumed pacing.

Josh motioned James to check the supply closet and office while he checked the freezer and walk-in refrigerator. Upon finding there was no one hiding they made their way into the bar and dining area. Josh stepped into the hall to the bathrooms and emergency exit. A sound from the men's bathroom drew their attention.

James readied himself to follow Josh when he opened the door. He was about to turn the doorknob when it opened and a young boy about ten stepped into the hall oblivious to the two men ready to charge into the bathroom.

"Freeze!" James yelled as Josh grabbed the boy's arms from behind.

Josh cuffed him noting how thin he was. "Who are you?"

The boy raise fearful eyes to him but remained silent.

"I'll take him across the street while you and Larry go through to see if anything is missing." Josh said pulling the boy alongside him.

The boy didn't resist when he walked him into the station. He put him in the interrogation room which doubled as their conference room.

"Do you need a bottle of water?" Josh asked.

The boy didn't say anything. He just stared at Josh confusion and fear shining in his dark eyes. In his estimation the boy hadn't eaten in a long while. His clothes were tattered and dirty and his toes were sticking out of his worn-out shoes.

Thinking the young man may not understand what he asked, he went to get two bottles and returned holding one out to him. Mistrustful eyes looked between Josh and the water. Josh opened it and set it in front of him.

The boy's small hand tentatively reached for it while watching Josh warily. Finally, he grabbed the bottle and nearly drained it before taking a breath.

"What's your name?" Josh asked again.

When the boy remained silent, he stepped to the door. "Kelly?"

"What can I do for you Josh?" she looked at the boy with compassion in her eyes.

"Would you ask James to bring a couple of burgers, fries and a large soda for the boy." He replied. "Also, see if you can find someone who knows sign language."

"You think he's deaf?" she asked.

"I don't know." He shrugged.

"I'll let James know, then I'll call Kevin. He knows Indian sign language, hopefully it will work." She hurried to call her brother-in-law.

Josh sat down across the table from the young man. "My name is Josh."

The boy made no sign he heard or understood him.

James showed up and put the food on the table and told Josh there wasn't any damage to the bar except the door. Other than that nothing was missing.

James delivered the food, then observed the boy, who watched with interest as Josh put the food in front of him.

"Go on. You can have all of it." Josh said pushing it toward him.

Still cautious, he took a French fry and stuffed it into his mouth. Before long he had nearly inhaled the food.

"Can you tell me your name?" Josh tried again.

The youngster looked at him still confused but remained silent.

"Do you have a name?" Josh had a sinking feeling in the pit of his stomach.

Still his question remained unanswered.

"Where do you live? Do you understand me?" Josh asked growing frustrated.

81

The boy was either ignoring him or he was a deaf mute. This was one time he had no idea what to do. He stepped into the hall and asked Kelly if she'd gotten in touch with Kevin hoping his Lakota signing skill would come in handy.

He closed the door and went to his office to grab his laptop. Returning to the room, he sat as the boy scarfed down the last of the second burger. Keeping an eye on him, he booted up the laptop and ran a missing person search. When he came up empty, he took a sheet of paper from his little notebook and printed his name and pushed it toward him.

The child looked at the paper with a frown then pushed it back toward Josh, before returning to the fries and drink.

Josh had no idea how to communicate with him. He looked up when Kevin knocked as he stepped into the room. Quickly filling him in he offered a chair to Kevin hoping he could get the boy to talk. He sat back and watched.

The young man watched with interest as Kevin attempted to communicate but showed no sign of understanding.

Kevin turned to Josh, "I don't think he understands."

"Well at least you tried." He picked up the paper with his name on it.

"Let me see that." Kevin held out his hand.

"I wrote my name down to see if he could read." Josh slid the paper over to him.

Kevin took the pencil and drew a house and two people on the paper then pushed it across the table.

The boy looked with excitement and pointed at the house, and spoke in a strange language, neither men had heard before.

Kevin and Josh stepped into the hall for a moment.

"You might call Frank, he's been all over the world, maybe he or your brother knows what he is saying." Kevin suggested as Joe and Archer returned from talking with Jillian.

"What's going on?" Joe asked.

"I got a big mystery sitting in the conference room." Josh told him everything.

After a long discussion, Josh decided to take the boy home with him since Larry wasn't going to press charges.

"I'll call Will and have him meet me at Frank's. They might know what language he's speaking." Josh said helping the young man to his feet.

After he had the boy buckled in, he pointed his truck toward Frank's house hoping he could help.

Josh parked in the drive next to Will's truck and killed the engine. He looked over at his guest wondering what his story would turn out to be.

The boy understood Josh wanted him to follow as he stepped from the truck. The front door opened before they stepped onto the porch.

As Frank ushered them inside he asked watching the young boy follow Josh. "So what's the problem you think your brother and I can solve for you?"

"I want to know if you can decipher his language." Josh told them the story.

Will sat in the den where he heard everything and watched Frank try to communicate with the frightened child. When the boy stared at him with no sign of understanding Frank turned to Josh in frustration, "How did you get him to speak before?"

"Kevin drew a house with people in front of it." Josh handed him the folded paper.

Frank looked at the drawing then gave it to the young man surprised when his face lit up and he began speaking excitedly.

Frank's brow furrowed as he tried to decipher the language but drew a blank as he turned to his friend. "Will?"

"I'm not sure, but could it be Creole?" Will asked.

"I'll call Jimmy LeBouf. Being from Louisiana he may know." Frank yanked out his phone.

"LeBouf." Jimmy answered his cell.

"Hey, Gator. It's Bear." Frank replied.

"How in the world are you?" Jimmy asked.

"There's a lot you've missed around here. Ginger and I now have twin boys and recently became foster parents to twin girls." Frank bragged a bit.

"Wow. You keep that up and you'll have your own baseball team." Jimmy chuckled. "How's Wolf?"

"He and his wife Samantha are parents to two boys and a girl." Frank told him.

"That's great. What can I do for you?" Jimmy asked.

"Our deputy found a child who doesn't speak English. Will thought he spoke some form of Creole. Could you meet us in Sheridan to talk to him?" Frank asked.

"I'll do you one better. I'm retiring and tomorrow is my last day. I'll come to Wolf Creek to visit for a few days." Jimmy surprised him.

"You're a little young for retirement aren't you?" Frank asked.

"Let's just say I'm ready and leave it there. Pick me up at the Sheridan airport Friday at one p.m." Jimmy said.

"Will do, have a safe flight." Frank replied before ending the call.

"Well what did he say?" Will asked.

"He said he's retiring and tomorrow is his last day. He asked me to pick him up on Friday at the airport in Sheridan." Frank said. "I can tell something's bothering him."

"I'm sure he'll tell us when he's ready. You know he hardly ever let anyone in his private life." Will said.

"At any rate, we need to take care of this youngster first." Frank changed the subject. "Where is he staying tonight?"

"With me until we figure out where his parents are." Josh answered. "Do you think Dillon might have some old clothes his kids have outgrown for him?"

"I'll call him now." Frank hit the button on his phone.

Dillon answered and asked his wife to gather a few things for Frank as he went outside to feed the animals.

Frank showed up for the clothes and told Dillon about the boy before taking the clothes to Josh's place.

Chapter Fourteen

After his long day of work, Dillon Smalley wiped the sweat from his brow as he parked the tractor in his barn. When he walked toward the house, he noticed Heather's car was gone. He went inside to find the children sitting on the couch in the den crying.

"Where's your mother?" he'd asked as a sinking feeling hit his stomach.

"She left." Twelve-year-old Andrew said holding a large manila envelope. "She left you this."

He put the envelope in the office then took the kids to the diner in town for dinner. What he didn't know was half the town knew she had left before he did.

Once the kids were in their beds for the night, he sat in his office chair staring at the envelope like a coiled snake ready to strike at him. He was half afraid to open it, but he had no choice.

Sliding his knife along the flap of the manila envelope, he pulled out a stack of papers and another smaller envelope with his name on it. Shoving the other papers out of the way he opened the letter.

Dillon,

I'm sorry but I can't live on the ranch any longer. It's not what I wanted to begin with, and you know this. However, I gave it a shot because I loved you. I tried to make it work for me. After gramps died last month, I found out he'd left his house in the Hamptons and an embarrassingly large trust fund in my name. I didn't tell you because I've been waiting for the opportunity to leave you, and it finally came.

Enclosed in the large envelope are divorce papers. I have the right to make you sell the ranch and give me half of everything you own, but I won't unless you fight this. I'm

*giving you sole custody of the kids, and I have set a trust
fund up in each of their names for when they turn eighteen.*

*I'm willing to give you eight hundred per child, which
comes to twenty-four hundred a month until they reach the
age of eighteen. I'll also pay for medical insurance on all three
kids.*

*I loved you in the beginning, but I've never wanted to live
on a ranch. I wish you all the happiness in the world.*

Heather.

Dillon sat back in the chair dumbfounded.
Never in his wildest dreams could he have imagined
Heather doing this to him and the kids. Shoot, he
realized he had misread how well they'd been
getting along and how happy the kids were since
she actually paid more attention to them. Now it all
made sense. All of it was an act while she planned
her escape.

Tomorrow he'd go talk to Frank while the
children were in school. Andrew was old enough to
understand what was happening, but Eric and
Abigail would be confused. He'd have to make sure
he never spoke a bad word against their mother, no
matter how angry he felt. The woman he loved just
flipped his world upside down and he had to figure
out how to right it again.

***

Frank opened the door to find Dillon waiting
for him to answer. "Hey Dillon, what's up?"

"I need to talk to you and Ginger." He said.

"Well come on in." Frank stood back to let him
in wondering why he looked as though he hadn't
been to bed yet.

"Who is it?" Ginger called from the den where
she was feeding Angela. The rest of the babies
played quietly in the play pens.

"It's me sis." Dillon swallowed the lump
threatening to choke him.

"What happened?" she asked frowning with worry as she put Angela in the play pen with Amanda.

"Heather left me." He handed her the letter and the divorce papers.

Frank read over Ginger's shoulder while her face grew stormy. "How dare she do this to you and the kids!"

"I shoulda tried harder to make her happy." He rubbed the back of his neck. "I thought she finally accepted things the last month or so. She really took me for a fool."

"Are you going to fight her?" Frank asked looking at the papers.

"If I do she'll make me sell the ranch. I have no recourse but to sign the papers." He shook his head.

"She can't make you sell anything. The entire ranch, including equipment and livestock are in a trust under your family's name." Frank said. "If I'm not mistaken none of it can be divided up without the consent of everyone in the family."

"I need to see a lawyer before I sign this." Dillon sighed. "Meanwhile I need a nanny/housekeeper."

"Sandra Walker is looking for a better job. She's tired of working at the bar." Ginger said. "Larry won't be happy that he has to find another waitress, but in this case he'll just have to make do."

"I'll stop by to see her." Dillon stood to leave with the weight of the world on his shoulders.

Ginger hugged her brother, "This might be for the best. You two fought constantly."

"Maybe." He hugged her back. "Thanks sis."

"Would you like me to have my computer whizz kid to look into Heather's financial situation? It might behoove you to see just how much she's worth now." Frank offered.

"Yeah, it can't hurt anything," he shook Frank's hand. "I'll see y'all later."

After he left, Frank called Abe.

"What's up boss?" Abe answered.

"I need all the financial intel you can get on Heather Swanson Smalley asap." Frank said.

"Will do." Abe said as keys clacked in the background. "I'll let you know what I find out."

"Thanks," Frank said ending the call.

Amanda started pulling herself up to her feet in the crib. "Look Frank!" Ginger pointed with a smile.

"I wish they would tell us something about adopting them." Frank grinned as Angela tried to stand but fell backward onto the mat in the pen.

Ginger giggled when she picked her up, "Someone needs a diaper change."

Chapter Fifteen

Charlotte Gunn looked up when Josh knocked on her door. It had been almost eight months since Frank and Ginger took in the twins. "Hello Detective. What can I do for you?"

"I'd like to know how your investigation into the Goines family is coming along?" he asked.

"I planned to call you later today. I've talked with Judge Odom and given him the file. There is only one thing that concerns us, Mrs. Goines anger issues." She said holding up her hand as Josh opened his mouth to cut her off. "I realize she went through counseling and fulfilled the court orders, but if I don't take that into consideration, I wouldn't be doing my job."

"She has become a model citizen since she married Frank. Through her counseling and his support, she is a different person. You can ask anyone in town how much she's changed." Josh defended Ginger.

"Like I said the Judge is going over everything. You still haven't found anything on the mother? No missing person report, or anything?" She asked.

"No ma'am. I have another issue though, and he explained about finding the young man in the bar." Josh shook his head.

"So he's an orphan too?" she asked.

"I don't know. I let him stay with me last night. He's with Will today until I get off of work." He replied.

"Since we don't have an orphanage I guess you'll have to do." She shook her head.

He stood up, "I need to get back to work. Thanks for talking with me."

Josh left her office praying that Judge Odom would see that Ginger worked through her past issues. While he walked back to his office, he whispered a prayer of thanksgiving for the little girls and asked God to grant their adoption into the Goines family. Then he asked for help finding information on his houseguest.

Kelly looked up from writing down a message for him. "Um. Hang on he just walked in."

She looked at Josh and said. "Kevin is on two."

Josh rushed into his office to answer the phone.

***

Jillian hadn't heard from her family for an entire week. Not that she was complaining, but now that they knew where she moved, she feared they would show up unannounced. Desperate to ease the worry in her heart, she saddled Rosebud and rode her through the pasture. She still hadn't seen all of her ranch. She knew Kevin would wonder where she went, but she needed to work some things out in her head. Mostly, she just needed some alone time.

She reined Rosebud to a stop on top of the large hill leading into the forest. From there she could see the creek running through her land. Beyond that, she saw the natural rise onto the side of the mountain. Something glittering in the sunlight caught her attention. After a moment of hesitation, she picked her way down the rocky hillside and across the stream.

The closer she got to the glittering spot the more trouble she had keeping it in sight. Finally, she reached a small clearing and found the remains of a man. Before she could get off the horse, Rosebud reared up forcing her to hold on for dear life.

"Rosebud!" she shouted as the horse bolted for home with her trying to keep from falling off.

91

Kevin stepped outside of the barn with Wild Wind saddled to go searching for Jillian. The woman was a greenhorn and had no business going off like that by herself.

He put his foot in the stirrup to pull himself into the saddle when he saw Rosebud galloping toward him with Jillian hanging on for all she was worth. Quickly seating himself in the saddle, he kicked Wild Wind into a gallop to stop the runaway horse.

Jillian's heart felt like it was going to beat out of her chest causing her to be short of breath. When Kevin reached her, he grabbed Rosebud's reins and pulled both animals to a stop much to Jillian's relief.

"What happened?" he asked tersely as he guided the horses back to the barn.

"I needed to clear my head and wanted to look at the rest of my ranch." She managed. "I found a dead man on the other side of the creek on the mountainside."

"What spooked the horse?" he asked helping her down.

"I don't know. It might have been the corpse." She said as Kevin steadied her on the ground.

"I'll call Josh so he can investigate, while you go inside and calm down." Kevin said.

Jillian didn't argue as she attempted to walk on rubbery legs. Why was she finding dead people all of the sudden? She'd been here almost nine months, she had found three deceased people. Thankfully, the twin girls she found were okay.

Kimberly looked up from the laptop when Jillian opened the door. "What happened?" she jumped to help her sit down.

"I found a dead man on my property." She said sinking into the chair.

Kimberly offered her a glass of water and sat across from her. "Where?"

"Across the creek up on the mountainside. Kevin is calling Josh." She told her.

Kimberly wondered about the woman who graciously offered them a home. From her point of view, she found dead people a lot. It didn't fit with what she knew of the woman.

Kevin left the saddles on the horses after cooling them down. He saddled Misty for Josh to ride when he showed up. He turned from the barn when Josh parked his truck in the drive.

Josh greeted him as he followed him into the house.

"Jillian's inside, she'll have to show us where she found the body." Kevin held the door for Josh.

Jillian's heart slowly returned to normal until Josh stepped into the kitchen. Just hearing his voice caused it to hammer against her ribs again. She realized she couldn't stop the feelings developing for the gorgeous man.

"Are you okay to show us where you found the corpse?" he asked.

"Yes." She nodded. "I don't know why Rosebud acted the way she did."

"I'll have my rifle with me in case it was a wild animal." Josh said helping her from the chair.

"So will I." Kevin said following them outside.

The threesome rode through the stream toward the place Jillian directed them to. Rosebud was fine with the other horses until they started fighting to get away from the area.

"Let's take them back to the stream and ground tie them." Josh suggested. "We'll go in on foot."

Josh suggested that Jillian stop about thirty feet away from the body and sit on a log. She watched the men slowly approach the corpse. Josh bent down to pick up a rifle and check the chamber. "It's been fired."

"I'm seeing some large mountain lion tracks. It must have surprised him." Kevin said.

"That would explain why his arm and leg are missing." Josh said thoughtfully. "I wonder if this man could be that young boy's dad?"

"If so, he might recognize the rifle." Kevin said.

"Only one way to find out. We'll have to call Doc and get a body bag to get him out of here." Josh moved to leave.

Jillian sat waiting on the two men to finish whatever they were doing when she heard a twig snap.

The moment she saw the mountain lion ready to pounce a scream split the air. A gunshot rang out just as the animal lunged for her only to fall dead a short distance away.

Jillian barely saw the cat hit the ground before everything went black.

"Jillian?" Josh rushed to her.

Terrified eyes fluttered open as he looked down at her.

"You're okay, the cat is dead." He assured her. "Now we know why the horses didn't want to come up here."

He helped Jillian up and they left to retrieve the horses and rode back to the ranch house. Josh called Doc and explained what he needed and they sat down in the kitchen to wait for him to arrive.

Chapter Sixteen

Josh stopped in the drive of Will's house. Once he was inside the boy saw the rifle and ran to him talking. His excitement confirmed his suspicion that the dead man was indeed the boy's father.

Josh glanced around and asked his brother, "Where are the kids?"

"Mom Andrews took them for the weekend." Will replied.

"In that case, would you and Samantha go with us to get him some clothes in Sheridan?" he asked.

Samantha answered before her husband opened his mouth. "Yes!"

Will chuckled, "I guess we're going with you."

It was early enough they had time for a trip to Sheridan and a stop at the western wear store.

The distinct aroma of fine leather greeted them as they stepped inside the building. After an hour, they purchased several pairs of jeans, flannel shirts, a good pair of boots, and a hat for the youngster. Samantha insisted they stop at the big box store to get underthings and such. She made sure he had a heavy coat as well to withstand the cold winters in Wyoming.

They stopped at their favorite steak house before going home. Conversation flowed between the brothers about Jillian's plans for her ranch.

When dinner was over, Josh drove his brother and sister-in-law home.

Later after the child had a bath and Josh finally settled him into Trace's old room, he watched the little guy fall asleep with a smile on his face. A sigh slipped from Josh's lips in frustration that he still had no answers to the questions running through his mind.

The DA felt he would be safe with him. Now that he had him set up with clothes and a room, he realized he was going to have to wing it, as his eyes finally closed in exhaustion.

***

Jillian soaked in her tub letting the fragrant bubbles slowly disappear. The hot water had cooled enough that she needed to get out. After drying off, she put on a tank top and shorts to sleep in.

Just as she sat on the edge of the bed, her phone buzzed.

"Hello?" she answered.

"Hey Jilly." Carol replied. "How are you?"

"I'm learning a lot." She said then proceeded to tell her everything she'd been through since moving to Wolf Creek.

"Oh, my! Are you sure you want to live in a town where everyone is dying?" Carol asked with worry lacing her voice.

"Not everyone is dying. It just seems that way." She chuckled.

"Well, I'm calling to let you know, Jeb and Lucy decided they are going to bring you back from Wolf Creek. Cal and I are coming too. We won't let them bully you into anything you don't want to do." Carol warned her.

"When?" She stood and paced the floor.

"We're leaving early the day after tomorrow. I didn't think it was fair that Jeb didn't want to give you any warning. We should arrive at the Sheridan airport around three p.m." Carol explained.

"Do you want me to pick y'all up?" she asked.

"No. Jeb has already reserved an SUV for us. Besides if you show up he'll know I called, I'd like to put off him finding out as long as possible." Carol declined her offer.

"I have two rooms upstairs you can stay in, but y'all will have to share." Jillian sighed.

"We'll see you then." Carol ended the call.

With a huge sigh, she went to check on the two rooms to see how dusty they were. She'd already furnished them but hadn't been cleaning them regularly. When she determined they would just need touching up, she went back to bed. Tomorrow, she would help Kimberly run through the house and make sure everything was presentable. Thankfully, Kimberly diligently kept a regular cleaning schedule.

When her eyes started to close, she wondered if Jeb would cause problems because Kevin was a Native American.

The minute her family arrived she would insist that her brother behave or he wasn't welcome to stay. She wouldn't allow him to hurt her friends.

Beams of sunlight awoke Jillian even though she wanted to sleep longer. Her mind wouldn't shut off for long last night waking her more than once. Why did she care about what her brother thought of her? Yes, he had more money than the rest of them, and he was oldest in the family now that their parents were gone, but she couldn't let him lord over her like he did the rest of the siblings. Unfortunately, she was the only one who stood up to him.

Forcing herself to get out of bed, she got ready for the day ahead. First she needed to talk to Kevin and Kimberly. They needed to know who was coming and what might happen. Today the older man Joe brought to meet her, Archer McKinley, would start work as a security guard. When Kevin related his story to her after the men left, she felt sorry for the guy. She was a softie, and happy she hired him.

97

Kimberly set a cup of hot coffee in front of her husband as Jillian stepped into the dining room. "Good morning."

She replied getting her own cup of coffee.

Kevin could tell something was bothering her and waited for her to talk.

"I'm expecting company tomorrow." She said with a sigh. "My brothers and sisters will arrive late in the afternoon."

"So we need to prepare the rooms upstairs, but I've been keeping the house clean so it shouldn't be too hard to touch everything up." Kimberly nodded.

"I'll help you, but there's something I need to prepare you for." She cleared her throat hating the fact she had to warn of her brother's prejudices. "My brother, Jeb, well, he's outspoken and prejudiced. I don't want you to take offense to anything he says. I don't feel the way he does and neither do the rest of my siblings."

"Don't worry. I've dealt with people like him all my life." Kevin assured her.

"I'm sorry you had to deal with jerks like that. I'll warn him if he doesn't behave he'll have to leave. If you don't need me, I'll start cleaning on the rooms upstairs." Jillian said.

The two women whipped the house into shape and began making dinner. Thankfully, she'd gone to the store and bought groceries the other day.

Kevin and Archer stepped inside for the lunch Kimberly had prepared.

"Man, it smells good in here." Archer sniffed as he sat down with Kevin.

"I'm giving you a heads up, I have family coming to visit tomorrow." Jillian said.

"You don't look too happy about that." Archer observed.

"I'm not, but I can't just tell them to go back home." She sighed with dread filling her.

"I'm sure everything will be fine. You're a strong independent woman." Archer grinned at her.

"Thanks Archer. So how is your first day coming along?" she smiled as her face heated.

"I'm happy. Kevin has some good ideas for keeping the place secure. We can even bar anyone we want from entering the ranch which is a great starting point." Archer replied.

"Too bad we don't have that set up already." She muttered to herself as she punched the bread dough she was kneading.

Chapter Seventeen

Frank picked Gator up at the airport and talked as he drove him to the safehouse that doubled as an office of late in Wolf Creek.

"So, why did you retire Gator?" Frank asked.

"Let's just say I don't agree with some of the decisions coming down from the top. It's better I get out now rather than later." Jimmy shrugged.

"I can see that. I've noticed some things too from some of my other contacts." Frank replied.

"Tell me about this boy." Jimmy changed the subject.

Frank told him all he knew about the youngster.

"Are you sure he's speaking Creole?" Jimmy asked.

"Well, no, Will picked up on the Creole and I agreed with him." Frank replied as he parked in front of the new office. "If you want you can stay at our house, but I'll warn you, we have the kids and they tend to get noisy for their middle of the night feeding."

"I'll stay here if you don't mind. It will give me time to figure out where to go from here." Jimmy declined.

"You can come to work for me, I can always use another investigator." Frank offered.

"I'll think about it. For now I just want to relax a few days before deciding anything." Jimmy said.

"Let's get you settled and then walk over to the police station and talk to Josh." Frank opened the door.

Shadow looked up from the report he was filling out. "Hi."

"Shadow, this is my friend Jimmy. He's bunking here for a few days." Frank told him.

"Welcome." Shadow stood and held out his hand.

"Thanks." Jimmy shook his hand.

"Is Hawk or Justice staying too?" Frank asked running the schedule through his head.

"Yes, they're on at the bar tonight. I'm just finishing the case you had me working on." Shadow replied.

"Did you figure out where the money came from?" Frank asked.

"The boyfriend. The police arrested her husband for nearly beating the man to death. Turns out if she would have waited a few more days, her husband's lawyer would've served her with divorce papers." Shadow told him.

"How did the man find the boyfriend?" Frank asked while Jimmy listened intently.

"The husband had a feeling something was up that morning. He said she was too nice to him. Anyhow, he delayed going to work and the boyfriend showed up to get her. They were going to leave town. The husband went after him when the boyfriend ran. That's when the wife called the police but not before the husband caught the guy and proceeded to teach him a lesson. The wife wasn't too happy when she found out he hired me to follow her. If I hadn't been there to pull him off the boyfriend, he would've killed him." Shadow explained.

"Take a couple of days to visit Star and Trace. You've earned it." Frank insisted.

"Thanks, I believe I will." Shadow agreed handing him the report. "I'll see you later."

After Shadow left, Frank led Jimmy to the room he would stay in while he was in town. Jimmy set his suitcase on the bed and turned to Frank. "Let's go see this little boy."

101

"You don't want to get settled first?" Frank asked.

"I don't have much to unpack and I'm curious about the kid." Jimmy shrugged.

"Okay." Frank turned to leave as Jimmy followed close behind.

They entered the police station and Frank asked Kelly, "Is Josh in?"

"Yes, Go on back." She replied.

Josh looked up from the report he needed to fill out but didn't want to. He knew paperwork was one of the most important things in policework, but it didn't mean he had to like it.

"Hey Frank, what can I do for you?" he asked.

"Jimmy's here and wants to meet with the boy." Frank stepped into the room with Jimmy close behind.

"He's with Will at the ranch." Josh said standing to his feet.

"We'll meet you there." Frank said.

"Will do." Josh settled his hat on his head.

Frank followed Josh out of the station and drove to Will's house anxious to find out if Jimmy could talk to him.

Will came out of the barn as they parked in his drive.

"Hey Wolf." Jimmy greeted him.

Will shook his hand. "Good to see you again Gator."

"Where's the kid?" Josh asked looking around for him.

"He's inside with Samantha. She's trying to fatten him up some. I have to say he has an appetite now that he knows we won't hurt him." Will explained.

They followed Will into the house and sat down at the dining room table where the boy was shoveling food into his mouth. He looked at the new man with interest.

"Hello," Jimmy tried straight Creole language with him.

The boy responded warily.

"What's your name?" Jimmy asked.

"Mat chew." He replied then rattled off excitedly.

Everyone else remained silent as Jimmy conversed with the child.

Finally, Jimmy turned to them. "His name is Matthew DuBois. He lived with his mom and dad deep in the bayou until his mother left him and his father. The father moved them into the mountains west of here. I'm guessing in one of the old-line shacks they used back in the day.

"Did he give you his father's name?" Josh asked.

"He just called him dad." Jimmy shook his head.

"What else did he say?" Josh asked.

"He's been alone for a long time. His dad went hunting and never came back." Jimmy replied.

"Yeah, we found his father. A hungry mountain lion killed him. We brought his rifle back and his excitement when he saw it confirmed it was his father's." Josh told him. "He has barely said a word since."

"He understands his father is dead and is scared of what will happen to him." Jimmy said.

"Well, he's staying with me since we have no place to put him. Will and Trace keep an eye on him while I work." Josh said.

"If you don't mind, I'd like to watch him while you work. It will be easier to talk with him if he's around me for a little while. It's possible he'll remember where the family stayed." Jimmy offered.

"I don't mind, if you think he'll open up to you." Josh shrugged.

103

"Now that you've worked that out, how about some dinner?" Samantha asked. "Will can fire up the grill.

"I'll go home and get Ginger and the kids." Frank agreed.

"I'll go pick up Jillian, if you'll call Trace." Josh said to Will.

Will grabbed his cell phone and placed the call as Josh left.

Chapter Eighteen

The next evening, Josh pulled into Jillian's driveway wondering who owned the SUV parked next to Kevin's truck.

He noticed Archer steadying a ladder that Kevin was on when he stepped out of the truck. From the look of it he was installing camera's.

"Hey Josh." Kevin waved.

"Hi." He replied. "Who's SUV?"

"Jillian's family is visiting." Archer said with a frown. "If that's what you want to call it."

Josh was about to ask what he meant when Jillian stepped outside followed by a large man. "Hi Josh."

Josh greeted her as the two men sized each other up.

"Who's this?" the man growled clearly unhappy about something.

Jillian rolled her eyes, "This is Detective Josh Wolf. He's a good friend of mine."

"You ain't been here long enough to make good friends." The man snorted.

"Josh this is Jeb Taylor, my older brother." She said with a frown.

Josh took an immediate dislike to the man, but for Jillian's sake he shook his hand.

"I stopped by to see if you'd like to join me for dinner, but I see you have company so I'll get going." Josh said.

"Don't leave. We've got plenty of food for dinner." Jillian pleaded with her eyes for him to stay.

"I don't want to impose." He said reluctantly.

"It's not an imposition. Come on in." Jillian stepped closer to Josh.

"Jilly, we have business to discuss. You don't want outsiders to hear our conversation." Jeb growled from the doorway. "We already have too many people in our business."

"I'm not discussing your opinion about my situation. I'm happy and I will not let you destroy it. Josh is welcome in my home any time he wants to visit. So get off my back and let us pass." She hissed.

"Maybe I should come back another time." Josh said as Kevin slipped up behind her brother.

"Is there a problem?" Kevin asked startling the man.

Josh barely contained the laugh rolling around in his chest.

"Warn a guy when you're behind him!" Jeb complained stomping into the house.

"Where's the fun in that?" Kevin called out after the man with a straight face and a twinkle in his eyes. "How's the little boy?"

Josh answered as he followed him inside. "He's okay. I feel sorry for the little guy. He's got no family now that his father is dead. I still haven't found out what happened to his mother. I'm not sure if he attended school either. I'm confident that Will and Frank's friend, Jimmy, can get more information on him. From what Jimmy says the boy is from the Louisiana bayou."

"We should search for the cabin he lived in. Surely there is some clue to who he is there." Kevin suggested. "It can't hurt."

"Although I agree with you, we have no idea where to start looking." Josh said as they sat at the dining room table.

After dinner, Josh asked Jillian to walk him to his truck. Jeb complained the entire time he was

106

there, so he decided to ask her out to dinner the next evening.

"I'd love to go." She accepted with a smile. "I'm sure my family can entertain themselves for an hour or so."

"Great, I'll pick you up at six." He said. "I'm sorry your brother is so cantankerous."

"He's the oldest and the richest so he thinks we should bow to his wishes." Jillian explained. "It makes it worse because I won't worship the ground he walks on. I'm the only one in the family who stands up to him."

"Good night Jillian." He said sliding behind the wheel of his truck.

"Good night." Jillian said standing on the front porch as Josh left. Her sisters ambushed her the minute she stepped into the house.

"Okay spill!" Lucy insisted.

"There's nothing to spill." She shrugged her shoulders.

"Don't give us that. That guy is hotter than sin and he looks at you like a kid turned loose in a candy store." Carol said.

"Did you miss the conversation when you got here about finding all the dead people? Josh is the detective in Wolf Creek. He investigates all that stuff." She sighed.

"So have you went out with him yet?" Lucy crossed her arms over her chest.

"Tomorrow evening I'm having dinner with him." She replied. "So y'all are on your own for dinner."

"You ain't leaving us here alone while you date some cowboy!" Jeb yelled.

"Jeb. You don't get to tell me what I can and can't do in my own house, well technically Kevin and Kimberly's house." She fisted her hands at her sides. "If you don't like it go to the B&B in town."

Kevin slipped behind Jeb again and said. "That's a great idea. My wife is pregnant and you are disrupting the peace we strive for."

"What?" Jeb jumped turning red with anger.

"Did you not understand what I said?" Kevin's face turned stony. "You've been here two days trying to push your wishes on Jillian. She tries to keep the peace, but when she doesn't agree you yell and stomp around like a petulant child."

"I've heard just about enough from you, injun!" Jeb bellowed. "I ain't taking orders from someone beneath me."

"Jeb!" the girls exclaimed at the same time as Cal shook his head.

"You sir are no longer welcome in my home." Kevin remained calm, but his eyes held fury like Jillian had never seen in him. "Get your stuff and leave, your sisters and brother are welcome to stay if they wish, but you will leave. You have a half an hour."

"If I leave, they leave with me." Jeb said turning to his siblings. "Get your stuff, we're going."

"I'll drive you to the B&B." Cal said. "But the rest of us are staying."

Jeb looked as though he would explode he was so angry. "Fine." He growled stomping upstairs to pack his things.

When Jeb returned carrying his suitcases, Cal followed him to the SUV. Before getting into the vehicle, he turned to Jillian. "Don't ever call me for help. If you want to live this way, I'll not lift one finger to help you no matter what you say."

"Don't worry Jeb. I can take care of myself." Jillian said saddened her brother was so hardheaded.

"I hope someday you'll see how wrong you are about things."

"Hardly, y'all are just like pop. He didn't listen either. If he had, the inheritance we received when mom and dad died would've been three times what we got." He argued.

"Goodbye Jeb." Jillian sighed. "I'm done arguing when you won't see reason."

After they left, Carol and Lucy sat across from her in the den. Kevin and Kimberly sat on the love seat.

"I apologize for my brother Kevin." Jillian said. "None of us feel the way he does."

"Don't apologize for how your brother feels. It's not on you." Kevin said. "I've lived with prejudice all my life, so it's nothing new."

Kimberly bid Jillian's family goodnight and dragged Kevin from the room to give them privacy to catch up.

Chapter Nineteen

Josh made sure Jimmy wanted to watch Matthew before he drove to Jillian's house. Because of his plans with her, the day seemed to drag on forever. He stopped and bought a dozen pink and yellow carnations before going home to get ready for the date.

After a hot shower, he took extra time to comb his hair the way he liked and after trying on several shirts, he settled on a green and white western shirt with pearl snaps to go with his best pair of black jeans. He finished off with his best pair of black boots to go with the black cowboy hat he only wore on special occasions. After slapping his best cologne on, he headed out to the truck ready to pick up the woman who had taken up residence in his dreams.

***

Jillian's sisters sat on her bed watching her choose the right dress to wear for her date.

"So, let me get this straight." Lucy said. "You met this guy when you reported the woman you found in the house. The next day he helped you get that truck, buy furniture, and take you to lunch. You don't consider that a date?"

"Nope. He had business in Sheridan and I needed help trading in that clunker of a car." She said holding up a yellow sundress while looking in the mirror. "He also knew where the best furniture store was. We only stopped to eat on the way home because we were starving."

"Oh, give me that!" Carol jumped up taking the dress from her. "You need something sexy to go out with that hunky detective."

Lucy beat her to the closet perusing her wardrobe. "You don't have anything in here to fit that bill."

Carol strolled to the bedroom door. "I've got a dress that will have him drooling over you."

"But I…" Jillian protested in vain.

Lucy grinned when Carol returned with a royal blue dress that while it wouldn't be something she picked for herself, she would definitely like to try on.

"Put it on." Carol shoved the dress at her. "It goes perfect with your skin tone and dark hair."

After she touched up her makeup, Jillian was ready for her date.

Josh parked his truck in Jillian's driveway anxious to get their date started. Cal, Jillian's brother, met him on the front porch.

"Hello, Detective." He greeted Josh.

"Hi, is Jillian ready?" he asked noting the seriousness in his eyes. "Is there a problem?"

"There isn't a problem unless you hurt my sister." He said bluntly.

"You have my word." Josh replied. "I will take good care of her."

"Then we're on the same page." Cal said smiling at him.

"I have to admit you surprised me. I expected your brother to be the one to warn me." Josh chuckled.

"I'm sneaky that way. No one expects the laid-back brother to scare the boyfriend." He laughed. "Come inside, and I'll let her know you're here."

Josh had never been nervous when picking up a date before. He paced the small foyer with the flowers he had brought for Jillian. Somehow he felt this date would define them as a couple or they would remain friends.

He turned toward the stairs when Jillian stepped off the last step. His mouth fell open when his gaze fell on her. Suddenly his mouth was dry and his tongue felt twice its size.

Clearing his throat he said, "Wow, you look amazing."

Feeling a bit shy, she smiled. "Thank you."

"Here, I brought you these." He said holding the flowers out to her.

"I'll put those in a vase for you, Jilly." Lucy said from behind her.

"Thanks." Jillian gave her the flowers after inhaling their scent.

"Are you ready to go?" Josh asked with his hands in his pockets. He wanted to reach out and grab her, but with her family standing there no way would he cross that line.

"Don't wait up." Jillian tossed over her shoulder.

Josh helped her into his truck before jogging around to the driver's side and sliding behind the wheel.

Jillian watched him start the engine and expertly turn the truck into the opposite direction. Soon he pulled out onto the road toward Wolf Creek.

Josh drove to The Wild Mustang for dinner and dancing.

"Where is your brother Jeb? I noticed he wasn't there." Josh asked.

"He insulted Kevin and wouldn't stop pressuring me to leave." She said as her cheeks heated. "I've never been so embarrassed in all my life."

"What did he say?" Josh asked. "I can't imagine Kevin being that upset about anything."

"He called him an injun. None of us could believe he did it. That's when Kevin told him he

had thirty minutes to pack his stuff and get out."
Jillian explained.

"I can't blame him. I would've done the same
thing." He shook his head.

They spent their time getting to know each
other. The more they talked the more the attraction
between them grew.

Josh seated Jillian at the table then took his seat.
The waitress asked what Josh wanted to drink
completely ignoring Jillian.

"I'll have a coke and my date would like?" Josh
raised a brow.

"I'd love iced tea please." She said.

"I'll be right back." The woman said turning to
leave.

"Sorry about that. My brothers and I eat here all
the time." He apologized.

"No worries." She said. "So, tell me something I
don't know about your family."

"My brother Will was a Special Forces
Lieutenant. He was in the military for eight years
before he left." Josh told her. "He came home a
few months before pop died. Mom died a few years
later. He kept the ranch running until Trace and I
could help out more."

"It sounds like you were still pretty young when
he came home." She commented.

"Trace was a senior and I was a junior." He said.
"We helped with the chores, but Will took care of
the rest of the ranch except on weekends, then we
all worked."

The waitress took their order and left them to
their conversation.

"I'm curious. What happened to Trace?" she
asked. "I noticed his face was scarred."

113

"He had a run in with a grizzly bear." Josh sobered. "We almost lost him, but he was too ornery to die."

"Did anyone kill the bear?" she asked worry furrowing her brow.

"Yes, Will and I emptied our rifles into the beast, but only when Shadow jumped on its back and slit its throat did it go down. We had to pull Trace out from under the thing. Shadow was a medicine man in his village before he left the reservation and used his Lakota voodoo on him. If he hadn't Trace wouldn't have made it out of the forest." Josh related the story. "Now he's a proud poppa of a little boy, Allen *Ohanzee* Wolf. Just so you know *Ohanzee,* means Shadow."

"That's cool." She said with amazement. "Is Shadow related to Kevin?"

"No, Kevin trained Shadow and Hawk on the reservation. He was the tribal law enforcement officer. Star, Trace's wife, is Shadow's sister."

"I was so angry and embarrassed when my brother showed his true colors last night," she said as her cheeks flamed.

"Although I don't agree with prejudice, they've grown up with it." Josh said. "They are proud and don't show their emotions much, but I can see in their eyes the pain it causes them."

"Unfortunately there will always be someone who has issues with someone they don't like. Just because your skin color is different doesn't mean you're any different. We all bleed red and have our hearts broken the same as the next guy." Jillian commented.

Their food arrived and they dug in when the waitress left.

"This is the most tender steak I've ever had." Jillian moaned.

114

"It sure is." Josh chuckled.

They continued their conversation through the meal and dessert. Josh took her to the dance floor for a few turns, then escorted her back to the table where Will and Samantha were talking to Hawk.

"Hello Hawk." Josh said seating her. "This is my girlfriend Jillian Taylor."

Jillian's smile grew because he used the term girlfriend. "I'm pleased to meet you."

Hawk excused himself to get back to work guarding the bar. Shadow appeared startling Jillian.

The man greeted them then turned to Will. "Has Frank heard from Elysa?"

"Not that I know of. Why?" Will asked as Josh's eyes flew to Shadow.

"I've called her two or three times this week and it goes to voice mail." He explained. "Considering the job she's doing, I'm worried about her."

"I'm sure if anything is amiss Frank will be the first to know." Will tried to reassure him.

"Maybe I'll stop by in the morning and talk to him." Shadow said as a table of rowdy cowboys ratcheted up a notch or two.

Josh didn't give Elysa's lack of communication another thought when he asked Jillian for another dance. They spent an hour dancing and chatting with Will and Samantha before he took her home.

When he helped her from the truck, he said, "I enjoyed our evening out."

"I did too." She smiled nervously tucking her hair behind her ear.

They walked slowly to the porch and she turned to say goodnight when he put his arms around her and kissed her.

"I'd like to see you again soon." He said looking her in the eyes.

"It would be my pleasure." She agreed. "I better get inside. I'm having the plans for my house drawn up tomorrow and getting the proper permits for everything we're working on."

"I'll see you tomorrow then." He kissed her again sending strong feelings through her entire being.

She watched him leave then jumped when the door opened and her two sisters stood there with anxious looks on their faces.

"Well? How did it go?" Lucy and Carol asked at the same time.

"It was great. Josh is quite the gentleman." She smiled.

"So dish!" Carol insisted impatiently.

"We went to The Wild Mustang in Wolf Creek." Jillian sighed happily. "We danced and visited with his brother Will and his wife Samantha. Then he brought me home."

"We saw that kiss he laid on you." Lucy giggled.

"Shame on you for spying on us." Jillian tried to sound angry but she couldn't.

The sisters enjoyed a cup of hot cocoa and teasing her before turning in for the night.

Chapter Twenty

Over the next few days, Jillian's family had to go back home. She had mixed feelings about their departure. Carol, Lucy, and Cal supported what she was doing and even wanted to buy some of the equipment she needed.

Jeb finally understood her need to help others and how happy she was. That realization came when he and Josh had a fight in the middle of the yard while she and her sisters were out shopping.

"Jeb, I've let you put your sister down, and berate her for several days because she asked me to let it go." Josh growled. "But I'm done letting you hurt her. You claim to be the Patriarch of the family, but you sure don't do it right."

"You need to step off! If you were the oldest in your family you'd act the same way." Jeb snarled. "I promised my dad I'd take care of the family and that's what I'm doing! Not that it's any of your business!"

"I don't care what you think you're doing, you will not push Jillian anymore!" Josh insisted.

Jeb lashed out with is fist, but Josh saw it coming. He swiftly dodged the hit, and had Jeb, who was twice his size, on the ground with his arms behind his back.

"Let me up!" Jeb bellowed.

"Not until you calm down." Josh answered with his knee firmly planted in the middle of Jeb's back.

Kevin and Cal stood back watching the event unfold. "Wow, Josh is lightning fast."

"He has learned the Lakota way. My blood brothers, Shadow and Hawk have taught him well." Kevin said with pride.

"Can you teach me how to do that?" Cal looked hopeful.

117

"It takes a lot of practice, and you are leaving with your family soon." Kevin replied.

"What if I stayed?" Cal asked.

"Do you want to?" Kevin knew to tread lightly.

"I've been thinking about it since I arrived." He shrugged. "I know Jilly would be happy, and I've needed a change for a while now."

"Talk to your sister then come see me." Kevin said. "I'll help you."

Josh finally let Jeb up on the condition he changed how he treated the family, especially Jillian.

"I want you to know, I'm going to ask her to marry me." Josh said watching the man turn red in anger. "Don't even start. It's Jillian's decision and hers alone and you better not tell her either."

Before Jeb could answer, the women returned with a truck load of equipment and supplies.

Jillian stepped from the truck eyeing her brother who looked close to exploding as Josh swept her into his arms and kissed her in front of everyone.

"Um, Josh? What brought that on, not that I'm complaining." She asked with her cheeks flaming.

"Just because." He replied with a grin.

"Okay, um, can you invite your brothers and their families out tomorrow for dinner?" she asked. "My family will be leaving soon and I want to have a nice dinner party."

"I sure will, I need to go." He hugged her and kissed her forehead. "See you tomorrow."

Jillian turned to her brother and asked, "What's wrong with you?"

"Nothin!" he growled and stomped into the house.

Jillian's mouth dropped open as she turned to Cal and Kevin. "What's going on with him?"

"Josh taught him a lesson and it embarrassed him." Cal laughed. "You shoulda seen it. Josh had him on the ground with his hands behind his back before Jeb knew what hit him."

"What were they fighting about?" she asked confused.

"He told our brother he was done letting him get away with badgering you." Cal replied.

"Oh my." Carol and Lucy giggled. "He got his behind handed to him didn't he?"

"Yup." Cal grinned. "Jilly, I need to talk to you for a minute."

"Okay," she said following him to the porch.

"Would you mind if I came back to stay?" he asked. "I mean permanently?"

"Of course!" she hugged him.

"I figure I can help with the ranch." He said. "I find I like the area and your friends too."

"You are more than welcome." She agreed. "We can build you a small house wherever you wish."

"Let's help unload everything, then we'll have dinner. I'm starved." Cal said as his stomach growled.

The next evening, Kevin and Cal were grilling the steaks, burgers, and hotdogs while the women were putting the side dishes together. The Wolf brothers watched the children while things were coming together for their meal.

Jillian had invited Frank and Ginger, Shadow, and Hawk as well. She had been making friends and wanted to include them.

Dinner turned out to be a wonderful time for all. Jillian had fun when the guys decided to play football and the girls cheered them on.

When they settled for dessert, Josh grabbed Jillian and dropped to one knee and asked her to be his wife.

Tears slipped from her eyes as she accepted his proposal. Everyone but Jeb cheered when Josh put the ring on her finger and kissed her.

The women gathered around her to look at the ring he gave her. The men slapped Josh on the back and grabbed drinks to toast the engagement.

Jillian watched Jeb step away from the crowd and walk toward the barn. She knew something was really bothering him so she followed.

"Jeb?" she called rushing to catch up with him.

He stopped walking and turned to face her. She knew her brother well and could see the regret in his eyes.

"I'm sorry sis." He sighed. "I was so intent on being like dad, I failed to see that you were happy and in love."

"Thank you for that." She said hugging him. "I am so happy. Josh is so much more than Terry ever thought about being."

"Yeah he is." He chuckled. "Terry wouldn't have stood up for you like Josh does."

"So, will you give me away when we get married?" she asked.

"I'd be honored." He said gruffly. "You're going to make a beautiful bride."

"I hope so." She said nervously. "Terry did so much damage to me I still have some things to work through."

"You know we have to get back to Arkansas." He said.

"Yes." She looked at him thoughtfully. "I'm going to warn you now, Cal is going to move up here to help me out."

"He always did love working with horses." He sighed. "I'm actually surprised he hadn't bought a ranch himself."

"So you're okay with it?" she asked.

"If that's what he wants." He shrugged.

"What did Josh do to you?" she couldn't believe how much he'd changed since their fight this morning.

"He explained that I didn't know how to be the Patriarch of the family. He punctuated it when I took a swing at him. That guy is lightning fast, had me on the ground before I lowered my arm." He said.

Jillian couldn't help but giggle. "I'm sorry. I wish I'd have been here to see it."

"If you had been, it wouldn't have happened." He smiled. "Why wouldn't you let him say anything? If I was coming on too strong why not just tell me?"

"Would you have listened?" she asked with a raised brow.

"Nope. Let's go finish celebrating." He held out his arm for her. "I want you to know, I really am proud of you."

Her throat constricted so she could only nod as they joined everyone else.

Chapter Twenty-one

Frank and Ginger stood in the courtroom with all their friends and family in attendance. Today Judge Odom would formally allow them to adopt the twin girls.

"I hear by grant your petition for the adoption of Amanda Grace Goines and Angela Dawn Goines. Bailiff, have them sign these papers," he ordered.

After Frank and Ginger signed them, the bailiff gave them back to the judge.

"You are free to go." He banged his gavel as he stood to leave.

"Everyone! Please meet us at our house for a party!" Frank yelled as they left the courthouse.

The line of cars driving to the Smalley/Goines Ranch stretched for at least a mile. It had been a year to the day that Jillian discovered the twins and their deceased mother. The entire town rallied behind Frank and Ginger to help them with their twin boys, sixteen months old, and the now one year old twin girls.

Ginger cried when the judge granted the adoption. She so wanted a big family and now she had one. Frank was just as happy seeing his wife finally overcome the shadow of losing her ability to have more children.

The party started and lasted until late in the evening. Everyone passed the babies around enjoying time with them. Amanda was already walking and Angela still wobbled but made progress. Willy and Frankie were protective of their sisters even at their young age. Frank suspected there was a tiny bit of jealousy there too.

Jillian left with Josh as the party broke up, while Cal rode with Kevin and Kimberly who had given

birth to a healthy baby boy, Kevin *Chaska* (eldest
son) Bright Sky. Jimmy had taken Matthew under
his wing while Abe, Frank's computer whiz kid,
searched for relatives in Louisiana.

***

White-hot rage rolled off the angry man who
watched from afar. He patiently waited for the
perfect moment to exact his revenge. Planning and
preparing took time and the day of reckoning was
drawing near. Soon he would strike one at a time
until each one of those responsible for ruining his
life paid the price he required. The sweet taste of
revenge would be merciless, swift, and painful.

***

Jillian grew frantic as their wedding approached.
She was more than thankful when Cal moved into
the house leaving Arkansas behind. When he wasn't
helping Kevin oversee the final construction of her
and Josh's new home, he visited Artie's ranch to
learn how to care for horses.

Kevin and Archer implemented the plans for
securing the entrance and exit of the property. At
Frank's suggestion they added more camera's
strategically placed on every building while Archer
learned how to work the computer system to
monitor them.

Kevin also oversaw the construction of the new
bunkhouses and medical building and other
outbuildings required for the business Jillian
envisioned.

Jimmy enlisted help from Shadow to find the
old shack in the mountains. They took Matthew on
several searches until they found the right one.
There they found an old family bible and a few
letters from family in Louisiana. After contacting
the family, Josh drove Jimmy and Matthew to the
airport to take him to his new home. The Wolf

family and friends had a party to bid the young man farewell the night before.

While in Sheridan, he picked up a few things Jillian asked for concerning their wedding. He delivered the items and took her to dinner at the bar. When they returned Josh helped Jillian from the cab of his truck and kissed her in the shadow of the barn.

"Three weeks, and we'll be husband and wife." Josh murmured.

"We need to get the furniture for the house and..." She said as he held her.

"We'll have the rest of our lives to finish all that. We'll be on our honeymoon for two weeks. Then you can worry about setting up our new home." He tightened his arms around her.

"Who will live in your house after you've moved out?" she asked.

"I'm going to allow Shadow to live there. Since Trace married his sister, he can be closer to her there rather than living in town." He said. "I don't think he and Hawk are getting along since he gave Trace his blessing to marry Star. Of course, he works out of town quite a bit, so it's a win for him."

"That is kind of you." She said resting her head on his shoulder.

"I want to apologize to you for the way I acted when we first met." He said changing the subject. "I was trying too hard to impress everyone with my new position of detective."

"I can't blame you for that." She shuddered. "Shoot, I'd be a little suspicious myself if a stranger kept finding dead people at every turn."

"I still shouldn't have acted the way I did." He said as he kissed her.

"I should get home, I have to be at work early in the morning." Josh reluctantly led her to the porch. "I love you."

"I love you too Josh." She answered and watched him leave.

She walked inside thinking for the first time in her life, she was happy. Kimberly met her in the kitchen where they continued stuffing invitations and addressing them.

"My sisters are arriving tomorrow to help with the final arrangements. I'm thankful you are going to be my matron of honor." Jillian said.

"You know if your sisters want that privilege I'll step aside." She replied.

"They know I couldn't choose between them, so they're happy to be brides maids. They understood when I explained it to them. I wish it were already here and over with." Jillian told her.

"It will be here before you know it. Since they're arriving so early, I thought while we were in Sheridan, it would be a good time to find all the gowns and your dress." Kimberly said.

"That's why they're flying in so early. Killing two birds... you know?" Jillian smiled.

"You are gonna be a beautiful bride." Kimberly said as Kevin brought their crying child into the room.

Kevin bent to kiss his wife and give her their son. "He's hungry again."

"He's always hungry, kind of like his daddy." Kimberly beamed at her husband.

"Y'all can go to bed if you want, I'll finish these last few." Jillian said with hope that she and Josh would be as happy as her friends were.

After putting the stamp on the last invitation, she boxed them up to take them to the post office in the morning. Slowly climbing the stairs to her room, that sense of doom assaulted her again. She knew Josh was the one for her. The peace she felt when she said her prayers at night confirmed what she knew. So, why did she feel something was wrong?

***

Kimberly drove Jillian in her new SUV to Sheridan while Samantha drove Star and Suzy on the long trip to the airport in her SUV. Thankfully, Kimberly knew Sheridan having grown up in Wolf Creek.

Jillian went over some of the things they needed to accomplish after picking up her sisters. That weird feeling in the pit of her stomach intensified the closer the day of the wedding came. She wouldn't allow herself to speak it for fear whatever it was might just happen.

"Turn right and follow the signs." Kimberly directed her when they finally made it to the airport exit.

After her friend parked the SUV she followed Jillian as they walked to the terminal hoping the wait wouldn't be too long. To her surprise, Carol and Lucy were waiting for her just inside the terminal. The sisters greeted each other with tears.

After a leisurely lunch they made the trip to the bridal shop. The woman met them at the door and led them to a round platform with mirrors on three sides placed between the two dressing rooms.

"My name is Maria. Let's go find some dresses in your size." The woman said turning toward the sea of white lace and chiffon on one side of the store."

Maria chose three while her sisters chose several more for her to try on.

Jillian began to feel overwhelmed after trying on several of the dresses, which her sisters gave their

126

honest opinion when she modeled them. The one dress that had caught Jillian's eye hung from the rack and she told Maria she wanted that one next.

Since she'd been married before, she wanted to have fun with the dresses. This was exactly what she wanted when she stood on the platform. The dress was white lace over white satin. The hem was cobalt blue fading up to white bodice with a sleeveless top and a long train. The veil had the same color fading effect.

The brides maids gowns were cobalt blue lace fading to white at the hem.

"That is going to be so cool when you ladies take your pictures." Maria commented.

The ladies left completely satisfied with their choices.

Chapter Twenty-two

Three days later, Josh and his groomsmen drove to Sheridan to get their tuxedoes. He really didn't care for all the fluff the women wanted, but he loved Jillian enough that he kept his opinion to himself. Her first wedding was at the courthouse, so he gave her the go ahead to do what she wanted.

Josh led Will, Trace, James, Jarod, Cal, and Spencer into the tuxedo shop. The salesman met them at the counter as his eyes lit up with dollar signs. "How can I help you?"

"We need black western cut tuxedoes with Cobalt blue handkerchief and neck ties for everyone except me. I want a white jacket with the cobalt blue lapel, necktie, handkerchief, and black trousers.

"Are you renting or buying?" the man asked hopefully.

"We're renting." Josh said.

After outfitting each of them, the salesman rang up their rental purchase. "You can pick them up two days before your wedding. The return date is two days later."

"Thanks." Josh said.

"Is there anything else?" he asked.

"That's all thanks." Josh said sliding the check across to him.

"We'll see you next Thursday." The man put the check away.

The men left the store for the steakhouse ready for dinner. After they sat at the table they gave the waitress their orders, Jarod asked if Jillian's sisters were married.

"I don't have any idea, that's a question for Cal." Josh nodded toward his future brother-in-law.

"Carol has been dating the same guy for three years now. Lucy is a free spirit. She hasn't met "the one" yet." Cal said.

While they dug into their food, everyone started teasing Josh. He took it in stride laughing with them.

Soon they were driving back to Wolf Creek. Josh dropped the Smalley brothers off at their house, then took Cal back to Jillian's. Disappointment clutched his heart that he didn't have time to see his future wife since he agreed to work the overnight shift. It was a small price to pay since Joe had given him the day off.

The women sat at the dining table putting bouquets and table decorations together when Cal walked in.

"Did y'all get your tuxedoes?" Jillian asked.

"Yes, we got exactly what your note described." Cal said.

"Good, that's one less thing I have to worry about. Wanna help us put these flowers together?" Jillian asked with a smile.

"Nope, I gotta check the horses." Cal left the room quickly with Kevin right behind him saying he was gonna check the perimeter for intruders.

The girls finished with the bridal bouquets and started working on the boutonnieres.

"Jillian? What is the line up going to be in the wedding party?" Carol asked.

"James is Josh's best man, then Will, Trace, Jarod, and Cal, while Spencer is the ring bearer."

"Kimberly is my matron of honor, then Samantha, Star, Carol, Lucy, leaving Suzy to be the flower girl."

"Where are we having the rehearsal dinner?" Lucy asked wrapping green florist tape around the boutonniere.

"Josh reserved the banquet room at the steak house in Sheridan. After our rehearsal, we'll meet there at six pm." Jillian replied.

Kimberly opened the wedding notebook to go through the lists again. "You ordered and paid for the cake. Larry the owner of the Wild Mustang, reserves Sunday and Monday for small parties. Ours is the biggest one he's ever catered."

"Have you been to the bar?" Lucy asked.

"It's really nice since Larry expanded the dance floor, put in a new stage platform, and added one hundred square feet to the front of the bar. The entire room is highly polished dark wood. From what Josh says, Larry has been raking money in hand over fist with the small parties he caters." Jillian said.

"I have confirmation on everything including the photographer." Kimberly checked off the bouquets, boutonnieres, and flower girl basket. "Next on the list is decorating the church and the bar on Sunday morning. Since the wedding is at six p.m. we should have plenty of time to do both. Josh and his family will take care of the bar's decoration, while we take care of the church."

The ladies finished and carefully packed the decorations. They sat around the table with glasses of wine and snacks.

"Just think a week from now you'll be Mrs. Joshua Wolf." Lucy said with a dreamy smile.

"What was he like when you met him Samantha?" Jillian was curious.

"Sweet. In fact, if it weren't for him, I wouldn't have married Will. I had a murderer stalking me and after Will proposed somehow the man gave the men tracking him the slip. I couldn't bear to think of the man hurting Will or his brothers, so I took my ring off and gave it back to Will." Samantha explained. "Josh found me and talked some sense into me."

"Wow! No one can tell you went through all of that." the ladies exclaimed.

"Oh trust me, between Trace's clowning around, Will's overall grumpiness and Josh's subtle humor, they kept me on my toes." Samantha laughed then told them about the skunk spraying Will.

"I'm glad Josh and I managed to get on the same page. The day I met him was his first day as a detective. I didn't like his attitude at all." Jillian giggled.

"I think most everyone who is truly happy in their marriages hated or had an intense dislike of their significant other." Samantha said. "Josh has been the quiet voice of reason since I've known him."

" Everyone was so proud of him as he worked hard training for the position. Kevin and Shadow taught him Lakota defensive arts. He's so good, Shadow is sometimes surprised at him." Kimberly told them.

"Who's this Shadow you're talking about?" Lucy's eyes lit up.

"He's Star's brother. The girl married to Trace, Josh's older brother. He's quite a guy." Jillian said.

"It's pretty funny when he slips up behind Trace without a sound. Scares him every time." Star giggled.

"Star, we should get home. I imagine Will and Trace are ready to have us take over watching the kids." Samantha said standing to leave.

Kevin and Cal came back in from locking everything up for the night, then walked Samantha and Star to her SUV. The rest of them slowly drifted upstairs to their rooms ready for bed.

Chapter Twenty-three

Thursday seemed to take forever to arrive. The appointment to pick up their dresses had gone well, and they stopped at the shoe store to pick up their shoes. Jillian picked up the gifts she had ordered from the jewelry store. Thankfully, the jeweler gift-wrapped them so the girls wouldn't see them.

For lunch they stopped by a small diner then had their hair cut. Jillian arranged for the stylists to drive to Wolf Creek Sunday afternoon to style their hair and give them mani-pedi's. Lucy worried they were cutting it too close between decorating the church and dressing for the wedding.

"Trust me, there will be more than enough time. The wives of the groomsmen and some of their friends will help set everything up." Kimberly said.

"That's how they roll in this little town. They love to party and will do whatever it takes to make it happen." Samantha added.

Jillian relaxed as well as she could but that nagging feeling still haunted her. She knew that Josh loved her and wouldn't leave her at the alter or anything, but the feeling something was wrong wouldn't go away.

"What's wrong Jilly?" Carol asked. She knew her sister too well.

"I've got a feeling something is going to happen." She answered with worry furrowing her brow.

"It's normal to have those kind of feelings before you get married." Carol said.

"I didn't feel this with Terry." She told her.

"You eloped with him, and if you would be truthful with yourself, you knew he was a mistake from the moment you met him." Carol reminded her.

132

"I know. I just want everything to go like it's supposed to." She agreed.

"Come on, let's take this stuff home and get ready for the bridal shower at Ginger's house." Kimberly said.

After dropping their belongings off at her ranch, they all met at Ginger's house for the bridal shower. She allowed Carol to drive since Josh was supposed to pick her up after they were through.

When they arrived, Frank was loading the boys into his SUV to visit Will. Samantha brought Suzy with her and left Dev and Spencer at home with their daddy. Trace also went to Will's with his baby. Josh was wrapping up a case so he would be free to pick Jillian up after her party.

Jillian and Kimberly arrived a few minutes early to help out if her hostess needed it.

Ginger opened the door holding Amanda. "I'm glad you're a little early."

"What can we do to help?" Jillian asked.

"Nothing. This party is for you. If you would hold Amanda while I finish setting up that would be great." Ginger said.

"Of course. Where's Angela?" Jillian took the little girl.

"She's inside with Samantha. Go on into the den, and I'll be right back." Ginger replied.

When the final guests arrived they started with a few games, then opened the gifts. There were so many it took an hour to open them all. Ginger broke out the refreshments as everyone visited with Jillian. Angela latched onto Jillian after Amanda toddled over to Kimberly. Suzy made the rounds to get her share of the attention.

"I'm glad Josh is bringing his truck to haul all this stuff to the house." Jillian said, "Thank y'all for the gifts."

"We'll come over tomorrow and help you set up your kitchen." Samantha promised. "It's cool that the contractor's finished your house just before your wedding."

"I'm happy they did. Josh and I will begin our lives in a new home." Jillian said happily.

***

It was too early to pick up Jillian so Josh stopped at Will's and joined in the fun with the boys. They played football much to the delight of the toddlers. Spencer tried to curb his enthusiasm, but accidentally got too rough with his little brother Dev forcing his daddy to have a talk with him.

"Spencer, I know you're having fun, but go easy on the little ones. You are bigger and can hurt them." Will explained.

"Okay daddy." He hung his head. "I'm sorry I made Dev cry."

"He'll be fine in a few minutes." Will said holding the sobbing child. "He's just scared."

"I think it's someone's bedtime." Frank picked up Willie who rubbed his eyes. "Josh can you get Frankie and bring him inside?"

The men gathered in the den of Will's large home after bathing the little ones and changing them into their jammies. Trace fed Allen while Frank gave the twins their bottle before bed. Soon the house was quiet while the babies slept peacefully in nearby playpens.

Will allowed Spencer to stay up for another thirty minutes while the men joked around with each other. After Will tucked Spencer in bed they turned to more serious conversations about Wolf Creek and its current residents until it was time to leave.

Josh parked in his drive to care for his horses before picking Jillian up. He stepped into the barn not bothering to flip the lights on. After caring for livestock since he was a child, he knew the placement of everything by heart.

When he finished, he turned to leave when a man jumped from an empty stall and clocked him from behind. Josh fell to the ground unconscious.

The man quickly bound his hands and feet together and dragged him into the empty stall. Then he dragged a bale of hay into the stall and sat waiting for him to regain consciousness.

Josh groaned as pain radiated from the wound on his head. When he moved he found he was bound hand and foot. As his eyes barely focused, he saw a figure sitting on a bale of hay.

"Who are you?" he asked, "What do you want?"

"I'm your worst nightmare." The familiar voice said. "You ruined my life and I've been waiting a long time for some payback."

"If you're someone I arrested, I assure you my actions were justified." Josh managed blinking to clear his blurry eyes.

"Oh, you didn't arrest me, but because of you I lost everything." The man growled. "You should've took the money and kept your mouth shut."

"Langston." Josh groaned. "You know you won't get away with this don't you?"

"I'll be long gone before anyone finds you." He chuckled. "I've been watching you for months."

Josh's cell phone vibrated in his pocket and the man grabbed it. "Huh. Jillian is calling for you."

"Don't answer. This is between us. She didn't even live here when all that happened." Josh winced.

Langston ignored the cell and dropped it next to him in the hay. "Time to exact my revenge and leave before someone comes looking for you."

135

Josh tried to protect himself but being bound he couldn't. The man delivered blow after blow with his fists and steel toed boots. The pain grew unbearable until the final blow to his head relieved him of all feeling as he fell into unconsciousness.

Chapter Twenty-four

Jillian called Josh's cell again wondering why he didn't pick up.

"What's wrong Jillian?" Ginger asked.

"I don't know, he's not answering." She laid the phone in front of her on the table as Frank arrived with their boys asleep in their car seats.

"Who's not answering?" Frank asked sensing her worry.

"Josh was supposed to pick me up thirty minutes ago, and he's not answering his cell phone." She explained with worry lacing her voice.

"I'll go check on him." Frank said turning to leave. "It could be he forgot to charge his phone or he's in the shower."

"I hope that's all it is." She said wringing her hands.

Frank parked behind Josh's truck figuring he was inside the house. When he got no answer, his gut told him something was wrong. He pulled out his cell phone and called Will.

"Hey Bear. Did you forget something?" Will answered.

"I'm at Josh's, he's not answering his cell or the door. You might wanna get over here." He replied. "I'll wait for you before searching for him."

"On my way!" Will ended the call.

In a matter of minutes Will parked beside Frank and jumped out of his truck.

"He's still not answering the door, and the barn is locked up tight." Frank said.

Will grabbed his key to the house and they went in together. After a thorough search they found nothing.

"Let's check the barn." Will said grabbing the key from the hook mounted by the back door.

Will unlocked the barn and turned the lights on. Nothing seemed amiss until they checked each stall and found him in the last one.

"I'll call Joe and the ambulance." Will said as Frank untied him and started working on him.

"Get my bag from the back seat." Frank tossed his keys to Will.

By the time Joe, Harlan Jackson and Buddy Armstrong, the new paramedics, arrived, Josh still hadn't regained consciousness. While Will and Frank filled Joe in on what they saw, the paramedics loaded Josh into the ambulance and left for the hospital.

"If you want, I'll get Shadow and Hawk on this." Frank offered.

"If we hit a dead end, I may take you up on that." Joe replied. "I'll get James to come out here with me and go over the crime scene."

"I'm glad he's one of your deputies." Will said as Trace slid to a stop in his truck.

"What happened? I saw the ambulance and hauled tail over here." Trace asked jumping from his truck.

Will filled him in and told him he'd meet him at the hospital. More than once he'd thanked God they had the new hospital in their growing town.

"I'm gonna go get Jillian, she's still waiting for me at the house." Frank said and backed his SUV up to leave.

Jillian paced from one side of the den to the other. Ginger knew she was worried and offered comfort, but it didn't help much.

Lights flashed in the windows and Jillian raced to the front door. She flung it open just as Frank closed the driver's side door.

"Where is he?" she asked looking past him expecting Josh to be right behind him.

"Let's go inside." Frank steered her toward the door where Ginger waited anxiously.

"What happened?" Jillian dug her feet in and wouldn't move another inch.

"He's on his way to the hospital." Frank said watching the color drain from Jillian's face. "I'll drive you over."

"Go, the kids are asleep." Ginger tiptoed to kiss him. "Keep me posted."

Frank led Jillian to the SUV and helped her inside.

He waved at his wife, then got behind the wheel and pointed the SUV toward Wolf Creek.

Will and Trace were pacing the waiting room and stopped when Frank entered with Jillian.

"Have they said anything yet?" Frank asked.

"No. They just got him hooked up to the IV's and oxygen when we arrived." Will replied. "The nurse said they'd let us know how he is after Dr. Carter finished his examination."

"I can tell you that he has a broken collarbone and some broken ribs. Whoever did this didn't hold back." Frank said.

"Whoever assaulted him was definitely angry." Will agreed.

"Wolf family?" the nurse called out.

"Here!" they all stood and crowded around the woman.

"The nurses are settling him into a room. I'll come back to take you to him. Dr. Carter will be in to let you know his condition." She informed them.

Twenty minutes later, They stood in Josh's room listening to Dr. Carter explain his injuries.

"He took a nasty blow to the back of his head resulting in a slight concussion. Three broken ribs on the right and four on the left. A broken collarbone, and broken wrist." He informed them. "He took quite a beating, but thankfully there is no internal bleeding, however he's going to have quite a few bruises. He's lucky not to have broken facial bones."

"How long until he's able to go home?" Jillian asked around a lump threatening to cut off her air.

"At least two, maybe three days." Dr. Carter said. "We're controlling his pain with heavy pain killers. It will take that long to give his body time to heal enough to cut back to milder pain methods."

"Thank you Dr. Carter." Will shook his hand.

"I'll be in to check on him before I leave this evening." Dr. Carter turned and left.

"Y'all can go on home, I'll stay with him." Will insisted.

"No, I want to stay." Jillian disagreed as her cellphone rang. "Hello?"

"Where are you?" Carol asked angrily. "We've been waiting to help unload Josh's truck for two hours."

"I'm at the hospital." She managed as her voice cracked. "Someone beat him up."

"Oh no! Do you need us?" Carol's tune changed in a split second.

"No. I'm staying here tonight. You can bring me a fresh change of clothes in the morning if you want." She declined.

"Of course. I'll let the others know." She agreed.

Jillian ended the call as Frank followed the others out of the room.

She sat down in the chair beside his bed and held his hand. Tears slipped from her eyes as she thought about their wedding in three days. First thing in the morning she would have to cancel everything. It was obvious that Josh would be in no shape to go through with it.

Bowing her head, she said a quiet prayer that he would recover quickly. Two questions played over and over in her mind, *"Who would do this to him and Why?"*

Josh moved slightly and she looked up to see him watching her. "What happened?"

"Someone attacked you. Did you see who it was?" She answered.

"Yes, I need to speak to Frank and Joe." He muttered as his eyes closed in sleep.

She knew the two men would be back to speak with him in the morning. Leaning back into the chair, she held his hand drifting into a light slumber.

Throughout the night, the nurse slipped in every two hours waking him and disturbing her from the few minutes of sleep she managed.

Chapter Twenty-five

The doctor came in just before seven a.m. to check him over.

"Good morning, Dr. Carter." She greeted him stifling a yawn.

"Good morning." He said looking at the chart in his hands. "We're going to start cutting back on the heavy drugs and see how he tolerates the pain. If he does well, we may let him go home tomorrow." He said.

"That's good news. Thank you." She smiled at him.

"You're welcome. I'll be back this afternoon to check his progress." Dr. Carter returned her smile.

Jillian watched him leave as her phone vibrated in her pocket.

"Hello?" she answered.

"It's Carol, how is he?"

"The doctor just said they're going to start reducing the high-powered pain medication. Hopefully, they'll let him go home tomorrow. We're going to have to cancel everything, because there's no way he can stand for that long." She explained.

"Don't worry about anything, Kimberly and I will handle everything." Carol insisted. "Just take care of Josh."

"Thank you sis. I'm glad you're here to help out." She said swallowing tears.

"I wouldn't have it any other way. In fact, after talking to Cal, I think I may move here myself." Carol replied.

"Jerry might object to that." She chuckled. "When are you two going to tie the knot?"

"We've talked about it but I haven't made any decisions. I'm still wary of commitment." Carol sighed.

"You have to let Thomas go, sis. I know he was the love of your life, but he wouldn't want you to live alone and miserable. He loved you so much, I know he would feel that way." Jillian said.

"I've tried Jilly. It's just so hard to believe he's really gone. Sometimes at night, I still reach for him and it hurts when I realize he's not there." Carol sniffed.

"I understand, and do you know what? Maybe if you do move here, it will help you deal with it a little better." Jillian suggested.

"I'll think on it a little more." Carol promised. "I'd better go and start calling these people."

"I love you, Sis." Jillian ended the call.

Later that afternoon, Josh sat in the hospital bed arguing with the doctor. "I don't want any more of that high powered junk. I'll deal with the pain."

"I can't force you, but I guarantee you'll want something before the night is over." Dr. Carter warned him. "Those ribs alone are going to be excruciating when you move."

"Then I'll take some over the counter stuff." Josh grumbled.

Dr. Carter turned to Jillian, "Do you think you can talk some sense into him? If he comes around call the nurse. I'll leave orders for a milder pain reliever if he decides he needs them."

"I can try, but he's a stubborn man." Jillian replied with a smile.

"I'll be back in the morning." Dr. Carter said before leaving shaking his head and muttering under his breath.

Joe and James knocked on the door distracting him from the building ache in his body.

"How are you?" Joe asked.

"Managing. I really need to be out there looking for Langston." He replied.

"Is he the one who attacked you?" Joe's eyebrows shot up.

"Yes, He said he has been watching me after he bushwhacked me while I fed my horses." He explained.

"Why would he want to hurt you?" Jillian asked.

Josh explained what happened with Ginger and the lawsuit the man had against her for beating him up.

"His lawyer paid me a lot of money to lie on the stand since I witnessed the beat down. The look on his face when I testified and gave the recording and the cashier's check to the judge was priceless. Langston lost the suit and spent a month in jail for lying to the court. The man even had to pay the court costs for bringing the suit against Ginger."

"So he took his anger out on you?" Jillian asked.

"Yes. I need to warn Frank and Ginger. He might go after her." Josh moved a little too quickly and inhaled sharply.

"I'll let him know. You stay there and get better." Joe insisted. "Now that I know who to look for, we'll catch him."

The men visited for a few minutes until Joe said he needed to warn Frank.

After they left, Jillian told him Kimberly and Carol were canceling the reservations and such for their wedding.

"I coulda made it." He frowned in disappointment.

"Oh really? And just how long would you be able to stand in one spot during the thirty-minute ceremony?" Jillian crossed her arms. "Not to mention, the dancing afterward? I doubt you can suffer through it even with pain meds."

"I'd still do it." He stuck his swollen jaw in the air.

"You're certainly stubborn enough to try. But do you want to have our pictures made with all the bruising on your face?" she asked.

"You have a point." He gave in.

"Don't worry about it, we'll just have to pick another date." She sighed. "I'm just happy you're okay."

"Are you sure you still want to marry me?" he asked reluctantly. "I'm in danger every day."

"Do I like it? No. Can I live with it? Even though I'll worry, I love you enough to deal with it." She said squeezing his hand.

"Have I told you how much I love you yet?" he asked in relief.

"Yes, but I'll never get tired of you telling me." She grinned. "Now, you aren't going to go back to your ranch until you can get around better."

"Will and Trace will see to my livestock. I've cut back so there isn't much to care for." He said.

Will knocked on the door and Samantha followed him into the room happy to see him awake and talking.

Chapter Twenty-six

The hospital released Josh the next day sparking an argument between him and Jillian.

"I can take care of myself." He growled.

"No you can't." she argued. "Your dominant arm is in a sling, your other wrist is in a cast, and you can barely take a deep breath without your ribs hurting."

"I'll be fine. Besides, you have too much going on at your ranch to stay here." He said.

"Kevin has it all under control. Don't forget Artie and Cal are there to help too. You may as well give up. I'm staying." She said glaring back at him.

Josh sat in the recliner wincing when he put his feet up.

"Uh huh." Jillian snorted. "You need me whether you want to admit it or not. I'll get dinner started."

He had just closed his eyes when someone knocked on the front door.

"Come in!" he called as Jillian rushed to open the door.

She skidded to a stop as Trace stepped into the house.

"Hey Jillian. Is he up to seeing anyone?" he asked.

"Yes, he's in a grumpy mood though." She closed the door and turned pointing toward the den.

Trace sat down in a chair across from his brother. "How are you?"

"I've been better, but I'll survive. What are you up to?" He asked.

"I'm checking your livestock. Will did it this morning and Hoss will take over tomorrow until you're on your feet again." Trace informed him.

"I appreciate it. Has Shadow been around lately?" he asked wincing from breathing too deeply.

"No, Frank has him out on an assignment." Trace shook his head. "Why?"

"I thought since Star is living in your new house, he might want to stay here when he's not working."

"Have you discussed this with Will?" Trace asked.

"Not yet. I don't think he'll have a problem with it." He shook his head.

"I think it's a good idea, and I know Star will love having him close." Trace said. "It will give him the opportunity to be a part of Allen's life."

"See it's a good idea." He grinned.

"I should go, Star's waiting to go to the grocery store. At least it won't take too long since the new grocery store opened. The two-hour trip to Sheridan was a pain." Trace stood to leave.

Josh and Jillian fell into a relaxed routine during the next few weeks. He accompanied her to the newly christened Silver Spur Horse Ranch. Everything was progressing nicely, especially after the town counsel okayed her plans. With her house completed, she and Josh set another date three weeks away. This time, Josh was determined to remain alert since they hadn't caught Langston. No one had seen him before he attacked Josh, and now it seemed as though he had vanished into thin air. Still everyone involved with that fiasco of a court case remained vigilant.

After Josh spoke with his brothers about Shadow moving into the main house, he made the offer to him. The man gladly accepted with gratitude.

Hawk still hadn't forgiven him for giving Trace his permission to marry Star, and they fought constantly. Even though Hawk had witnessed how much Star loved her husband, he couldn't let it go.

A few nights after Shadow moved into his new home, he walked across the road to visit Frank. No one had heard from Elysa for weeks. The feeling something was wrong grew stronger every day.

"Come on in Shadow." Frank greeted him at the door.

"I just dropped by to see if you've heard anything from your sister." He asked stepping inside their home.

"No. I can't even go look for her since she didn't let me know where they were going." Frank shook his head. "I've got Abe tracking her down. Hopefully, he'll find something."

"I'll go track her down if he comes up with anything." He said.

"Why are you so worried about my sister?" Frank asked with a frown.

"I like her and would love the opportunity to date her." He shrugged.

"Just take it easy for now." Frank hid a smile. He knew Shadow would make a good husband, but worried Elysa was too free-spirited for him. If they did get together he knew there would be many arguments about it.

"I hear you're moving into the Wolf's main house." Frank changed the subject.

"Yes, Josh is moving in with Jillian after they get married." Shadow explained.

"Have they settled on a date? I know it's going to be hard on Josh until his broken bones heal." Frank asked.

Shadow answered and talked for a few more minutes then left feeling worse than when he stopped in. He could tell Frank was worried too and hoped that he would allow him to track her down if Abe failed to find her trail.

Chapter Twenty-seven

Josh felt well enough to do desk duty but wasn't happy about it. Joe insisted he stay at the station when anything came up. He also knew that Joe only agreed because Josh grew bored with nothing to do. It was Thursday, and it seemed to drag on. Sunday he and Jillian would attempt to have the wedding Langston had ruined by attacking him.

"Hello?" he heard someone call out. Kimberly had stepped out to lunch leaving him alone in the station.

"I'll be right there." He called out.

Slowly making his way to the front desk, he found a stranger standing inside the door.

"How can I help you?" he asked the man who looked like a vagrant.

"I have a message for Frank Goines. Do you know where I can find him?" the man asked warily.

"I can take that if you want." He replied.

"No, I was told to give it to him personally." The man insisted.

"Okay, if you have a seat I'll give him a call." Josh moved behind the desk to pick up the phone.

Frank answered and told Josh he'd be there in ten minutes.

Josh told the man Frank was on his way, then asked if he would like some coffee.

"Nope, I just want to give the message to Frank and leave." The man responded.

Josh answered another phone call and radioed James to check out the complaint.

Frank stepped into the station spotting the man right away.

"I'm Frank Goines, how can I help you?" he asked.

"I was told to give you this message." The man held out an envelope. "I'll be going now."

"Wait just a minute. I might need to send a reply." Frank's gut twisted as he opened the envelope and scanned the note.

Without a word he rushed out of the door and spewed gravel as he gunned his truck.

"Who are you and what was in that note?" Josh asked as Joe came in.

"My name is Bob. Some man gave that note to me while I was sitting in the park at Sheridan. He gave me fifty dollars to bring the note here, he drove me to the outskirts of town and dropped me off."

"Did you know the man?" Josh interrogated him.

"No. I never seen him before in my life." Bob shook his head.

"Can you describe him?" Josh asked wishing Samantha was there.

"Yep." He said.

"Will you wait here until I can get my sketch artist here?" Josh asked.

"I guess so. Got no place to be anyhow." Bob settled into a chair while Josh made his call.

"Hello?" Samantha answered the phone.

"Sammi, it's Josh," he replied. "Can you take a few minutes to come and make a sketch of someone for me?"

"If you can wait until I drop the kids at mom's." she replied. I'll be there in half an hour."

"See you then." Josh ended the call.

"What's going on?" Joe asked stepping into the station.

Josh explained everything and Joe decided to drive out to Frank and Ginger's to ensure they were okay.

***

Ginger had just put her children down for their naps and proceeded to clean the dishes left from feeding the twins. While washing the counter, she looked out of the window toward the barn. The corral gate stood open, alarming her. Hurrying outside, she closed the gate relieved to see the two horses were still inside.

As she turned to go back to the house, a noise in the barn drew her attention. She figured one of her brothers had slipped inside and was trying to scare her. Cautiously stepping into the near dark barn, she called out, "Come on out you've had your fun."

"That's where you're wrong." A raspy voice replied from behind her.

A vicious chill raced down her spine, but she couldn't quite place who the person was. She turned toward the voice and realized it was Langston, the man she beat up when he put his hands on her without permission. The altercation was much worse than she'd intended because she believed Frank cheated on her after seeing photos of him posing with a woman from his past.

"What do you want?" she managed.

"Payback." He growled. "You and your friends ruined my life. I can't even get a job because of you! Now I have people after me because I can't pay the money I owe them."

"It ain't my fault you have a gambling problem." Ginger fisted her hands at her sides. "You're the idiot that didn't stop while you were ahead and went into debt."

"Enough!" he took a menacing step toward her. "Turn around so I can tie you up. Give me any trouble and I'll go after your children!"

Ginger had no choice but to comply. She would do anything to protect her family, including giving her life. Two years ago, she would have taken the creep down all on her own, but there was too much at stake to do anything foolish.

Oh how she wished Frank hadn't left five minutes ago, he kissed her and said he would be back later.

"Where are the keys to your SUV?" he asked.

"In the kitchen next to the door on the key rack." She replied.

"I'll be right back. You just sit there and wait for me." He stepped out of the barn.

Ginger hoped he wouldn't go after her babies and prayed for God to watch over all of them as she struggled against the ropes binding her.

Langston came back, jerked her to her feet and led her to the SUV. He shoved her inside and ran around to slide behind the wheel. He started the engine and peeled out of the drive onto the main road away from Wolf Creek.

Dillon closed his door and locked it. He turned to get into his truck when he saw Ginger's SUV speed past kicking up dust in its wake.

Sensing something was wrong, he dashed to his truck and gunned the engine. He tore out of his driveway and followed her. Yanking out his phone, he hit the speed dial.

"Hello?" Frank answered sounding panicked.

"Frank, it's Dillon, Ginger just flew by heading north. Is there some reason for it?"

"Yes, Langston sent me a note at the police station. He said he was taking Ginger and he'd be in touch." Frank quickly explained. "I'll call someone to watch the kids, do you have them in your sights?"

"Yes, I'm close enough that I can see the trail of dust they're leaving behind them." Dillon told him. "I'll stay with them until you can catch up."

"I'm on my way. Whatever you do don't lose them." Frank ended the call and dialed Star.

When Star answered the phone, Frank didn't give her any time to greet him. "Star, I need you to go to my house and stay with the kids. I don't have time to explain, but they're there by themselves."

"I'll be right over." She promised picking up her baby and putting him in his cradle board Shadow had made her. Rushing outside, she told Trace what was going on and jumped on Silver riding bareback across the road. She put the horse in the corral with the other horses and rushed inside. All was quiet when she stepped into the babies rooms to check on them. Thankfully, they were sound asleep. Settling in the den, she sat back in the rocker and tended to her own child. Although she was curious about why the babies were alone, and where their mother was. She knew Ginger would never purposely leave them unattended.

***

Frank could see Dillon's truck ahead and glanced at his speedometer. He was traveling at ninety miles an hour and Frank increased his speed to well over a hundred to pass him.

Dillon watched Frank leave him in a cloud of dust and increased his speed. If his sister was in her SUV he wanted to know what was going on.

The two trucks began to gain ground when the unthinkable happened. Frank was close enough to read the license plate clearly. Then the SUV swerved as a big buck flew into the air over the top of the vehicle. Frank dodged it and watched his wife's SUV flip. He counted four times as it rolled winding up in the field.

He skidded to a stop at the same time Dillon did. Simultaneously the two men jumped from their trucks and ran to check on Ginger.

Ginger had no way of holding on to the door since the rope around her wrist prevented it.

Langston didn't put her seat belt on so she was desperately trying to remain seated as he took the curves of the road at breakneck speed. Everything went in slow motion when she saw the big buck jump in front of her SUV. The huge animal flew into the air landing on her windshield before bouncing over the top. That's when she caught sight of her husband's truck dodge the animal, barely missing it. In the next instant, her body sailed around inside of the vehicle. Langston's airbag knocked him out when it deployed. When the SUV came to a stop she landed on the roof.

"Ginger!" she barely heard Frank's voice.

A slight moan slipped from her lips as she fell into oblivion.

Frank told Dillon to call the police and ambulance while he grabbed his first aid kit. He didn't have a backboard to immobilize her, so he improvised. Dillon had some small pieces of scrap plywood in the back of his truck along with some tie down straps. Between the two of them, they slid the smallest piece of plywood under her and Frank tied her to the board with the straps.

Gently pulling her from the wreckage, they carried her back to the road. Joe pulled up with the ambulance close behind.

Frank handed Ginger over to their care, then ran back to get Langston. He was fully intent on murdering the man if he survived. Dillon followed with the same intentions. Joe stepped between them and shook his head. Even though he was wearing his seatbelt, he suffered severe head trauma.

The State Trooper pulled up to take over the scene since Joe was out of Wolf Creek authority.

Frank and Dillon gave their statement before leaving for the hospital. On the way, Frank called

Trace and asked if Star would stay to care for his children after informing him of the accident.

Chapter Twenty-eight

Jillian helped Carol hang the curtains in the living room of the new house she and Josh would move into next week. Sunday they would finally have their wedding, barring any unforeseen circumstances. Friday, they would have their rehearsal again, then another dinner for the wedding party.

Since the traditional parties had already taken place, Saturday was free to move Josh's things into their new home, while she and the girls handled last minute details.

"After we're finished with the curtains, we need to scrub everything down before the men deliver the rest of our furniture." Jillian said.

"I can't believe you're getting married on Sunday." Lucy said as she entered the room. "I really want to see that guy Shadow again. He is one hot dreamboat."

"I hate to burst your bubble, but he has eyes for his boss's sister Elysa." Kimberly sat down to nurse her son. "I overheard him talking to Frank about her. They haven't had any contact with her since she took a new job."

"Was it dangerous or something?" Carol asked.

"From what Josh said, she follows some guy around taking pictures of homeless people while he interviews them." Jillian said. "He and Elysa dated for a few months when she first arrived but decided to remain friends."

"So he's hung up on her then." Lucy's face fell. "Oh well, maybe there will be some other guys at the wedding."

"Trust me there will be." Kimberly smiled. "Brock's brother Jarod just broke up with his girlfriend. At least that's what Kelly told me."

"Oh, is he good looking?" Lucy perked up.

"Yes he is. There are also a few other single men sure to be there." Kimberly put the child over her shoulder to burp him.

"Do you really want to start something with a guy when you're going home in a few days?" Jillian asked.

"I'm not looking to get married sis. I just want a date for the reception." She held up her hands. "There ain't no way I'm going to date anyone seriously until I have time to have them thoroughly investigated."

"I get it. You want someone who loves you for you and not your money." Jillian smiled. "I didn't tell Josh everything about my financial situation yet. He's in for a big surprise when I tell him."

"No offense dear sister, but I suspect he has an idea that you're rich. You've done so much with your money on this ranch." Carol chuckled. "I really don't think he cares about it. Everyone can tell he loves you just by watching him when you're around."

Kimberly's cell phone rang in the middle of their discussion. Jillian hurried to her side when her face morphed into devastation. Tears fell from her cheeks as she ended the call.

"What's wrong Kimberly?" Jillian asked.

"Ginger, Kelly's sister-in-law, was in a really bad accident." Kimberly replied getting up. "I gotta get to the hospital."

"I'll drive you since Kevin is out plowing my wheat fields." She insisted.

"We'll watch little Kevin for you." Lucy and Carol offered.

"Thanks." Kimberly said as she and Jillian walked to the front door.

***

Josh looked up when Joe stepped into his office. "What's wrong?" he asked.

157

"Langston kidnapped Ginger." Joe said giving him the rundown of what happened.

"Is Ginger okay?" Josh jumped to his feet.

"She's in the hospital. I don't know anything more since I stayed with the state trooper who took over since they were out of the county by the time Frank caught up with them." Joe replied. "Go on over and be with your family. If she's able to give her statement you can get it. I'm going to fill out the paperwork."

Joe didn't need to ask him twice. He was gone before Joe made it to his office.

Still unable to move swiftly down the street, Josh hurried as fast as his body would allow. Jillian saw him and stopped, "Hey, get in we're headed to the hospital."

Josh slowly climbed into her truck, "You've heard?" he asked as he closed the door.

"Yes, Kimberly just found out." Jillian replied.

After she let Josh and Kimberly out at the entrance to the ER, she parked and ran inside. She might not know Ginger very well but she knew enough to like her. Besides, Josh grew up with her and she wanted to support him.

When she went inside she found the waiting room full of people. Over the last year she'd managed to place faces with names and knew most everyone in the room. Josh sat next to James and Kimberly and scooted over to allow her to sit with him.

"Have they heard anything?" she whispered to Josh.

"No, James said her injuries were severe. The guy who kidnapped her is dead." Josh answered.

"So it's the same guy who hurt you?" she knew instinctively he was.

"Yes." Josh grimaced. "At least we have one less maniac running around loose."

Frank stood next to the door waiting for the doctor to tell them something. It was one more thing to worry about. With his sister missing, a few issues at work, and now this? He had no idea if he could handle much more. Shoot, even when he was in the military, he hadn't had this much stress.

"Frank?" Dr. Sims tapped him on the shoulder. "She's fine. Her body took a beating in that accident and she has a concussion. I suspect she's got a few pulled muscles and a lot of bruises. God had his hand on her or she wouldn't have made it out of that accident from what the paramedics told me. I want to keep her overnight for observation."

"Can I stay with her?" he asked swallowing the lump of relief in his throat.

"I don't see why not." Doc Sims smiled. "You're gonna need an army to take care of your babies."

"I got this." Frank said.

"Good." Doc turned to leave. "Y'all can see her tomorrow, she needs to rest for now."

Samantha sat down with the women in the room and decided on a schedule for watching the Goines twins, as they became known in the small town. She then set up a meal train to feed the family until Ginger could get around better.

Everyone left Frank to sit with his wife assuring him they would take care of his family.

Frank looked up to the heavens thanking God for meeting Will all those years ago. The friendship they had formed through tough missions eventually led him to Wolf Creek. Now the entire community had become family.

He sat down next to his wife's bed and held her hand while she slept. Because he knew Samantha was in charge of his babies, he didn't worry about them, leaving him free to concentrate on his wife.

Chapter Twenty-nine

Sunday morning found Jillian stretching in her new bed she would share with her husband from this day forward. A knock on her front door made her scramble to get her robe on. Hurrying downstairs, she looked out of the window and opened the door to Kimberly and her sisters.

"Y'all are a bit early aren't you?" She asked. "I haven't even had my coffee yet."

"We have a lot to do today." Carol said.

"First, breakfast." Lucy put a box of pastries on the kitchen island. "We've all been starving ourselves for the last few weeks to fit into our dresses. Now we can indulge again."

Jillian had a cream cheese Danish with her coffee, then went upstairs to shower and dress. Soon the women loaded all their dresses and other things they would need to ready themselves for the wedding. Carol insisted she drive so Jillian could relax.

Everyone chattered with excitement as Carol parked beside the church and watched the last of the morning parishioners leave. The pastor carried the few boxes of decorations inside then went to his home for lunch.

In no time the women had the inside of the church decked out with flowers and ribbons. Then they sequestered themselves to the classroom that doubled as the bride's dressing room.

Carol began working on the girls' makeup, while Lucy put everyone's hair in curlers. They had four hours to make themselves look like princesses to Jillian's queen.

***

Josh and his groomsmen arrived one hour before the wedding to change into their tuxedoes.

They had helped Larry set the bar up for their reception afterward. Now they were grooming themselves and straightening ties, shining shoes, and making sure they looked good enough to stand with Josh.

Josh grew more anxious as the minutes passed until he would set eyes on his bride for the first time in two days. There were so many things for the wedding to take care of, and then helping Frank and Ginger out, they barely had time to talk on the phone.

"Calm down Josh." Will slapped his shoulder. "It'll be over before you know it."

"I'm happy I can put my arm in the jacket. I was afraid I'd have to wear that sling." He replied. "Doc said I was good to go."

"Guy's? It's time." Kevin stuck his head into the room.

Josh took a deep breath and followed the men into the sanctuary filled with friends and neighbors. He took his place as his groomsmen waited in the foyer to escort the bridesmaids down the aisle.

***

Jillian took one last look in the mirror when her brother knocked on the door. Kimberly opened it to allow him into the room.

"Are you ready?" he asked swallowing the lump in his throat. His little sister looked so beautiful in her dress, but it paled against the expression of love and excitement shining from her face.

"Yes." She hugged him then watched the girls file out of the room in the designated order they were to walk down the aisle.

She took her brother's arm and followed Kimberly from the room. Jeb stopped just out of sight and they watched Spencer herd his sister Suzy down the aisle as she dropped flower petals along the path.

Kimberly and James took their places and the music changed. Everyone stood to their feet and turned to watch her make her entrance. After a deep breath, she and her brother took the first step toward the man she loved.

When Josh saw his love step from the shadows, his breath hitched. Watching her glide effortlessly down the aisle, slayed him. Never in his life had he seen a more beautiful bride.

Jeb stopped in front of Josh and put his sister's hand in his. "You hurt my baby sister and no one will find your body." He whispered.

"I won't." Josh replied. This was the first time Jeb actually scared him.

The pastor began the ceremony and the appropriate time stood back as Jillian and Josh poured different colored sand into a vase symbolizing their joining as one. On that table were pictures of their parents. The song "Grow Old With Me" by Mary Chapin Carpenter played softly in the background.

They stepped back to their places in front of the pastor and exchanged their vows and rings. They turned as the pastor pronounced them Mr. and Mrs. Josh Wolf in the wake of the long kiss Josh planted on her.

They lined up at the exit to shake hands with the guests as they left for the bar while the photographer took their pictures. Their unique clothing allowed him to let "his creative juices to flow" as he put it.

When they finally stepped into the bar, most everyone was sitting with their drinks waiting for them to arrive.

Grateful for a moment to sit, Jillian slipped her high heels off under the table. Josh sat next to her digging into the delicacies Gary, the cook for the bar, had provided.

Champagne flowed freely throughout the evening. The couple shared their first dance, then Will confiscated her for one dance while Carol shared one with Josh.

"Welcome to the family." Will said smiling down at her. "Thank you for making my brother so happy."

"It's my pleasure and thank you." She replied happily as her brother cut in.

"Well, you're a married woman again." Jeb said. "Just so you know, Josh is a good man."

"Yeah, I think so." She smiled up at him. "It just took him knocking some since in you before you could see it."

"I know." Jeb grimaced. "I maybe a bit overbearing and hard to get along with, but I'm big enough to admit when I'm wrong."

"And I'm proud of you for being the kind of man Dad raised you to be." Jillian said.

The time came to cut the cake and Jillian smushed it in Josh's face amid laughter. They drank their champagne toast then sat back down to eat the rest of their slice of cake. While the best man and matron of honor toasted the happy couple.

Before long, Josh threw the garter and Jillian tossed the bouquet to the waiting singles. Carol wound up with the bouquet and Jarod caught the garter.

Birdseed pelted them as they ran toward his truck the men decked out with streamers, shoe polish and tin cans they tied to the trailer hitch.

When they left, the party slowly broke up leaving the few who were responsible for clean up to do their jobs.

Epilogue

Frank put the babies to bed, then went to help Ginger upstairs. When he entered the den, lights flashed in the front window.

He opened the door just as Josh and Jillian stepped onto the porch.

"Aren't you two supposed to be on your honeymoon?" he grinned shaking Josh's hand.

"We wanted to stop and check on Ginger before leaving." Josh said.

"I wanted to bring y'all some cake and a bottle of champagne. I know how much Ginger wanted to be there." Jillian explained.

"That's mighty kind of you Jillian." Frank opened the door wider.

They followed him to the den after he closed the door.

Ginger carefully moved to sit up when they walked into the room.

"Don't move from your spot." Josh insisted. "We just wanted to drop off some cake and champagne for you. I know you can't drink the champagne because of your painkillers, but you'll be off of those in no time."

"Thank you." She looked up with moist eyes. "I really wanted to be there."

"I somehow feel responsible for you getting hurt." Josh said when she raised a hand to stop him.

"Josh, you didn't cause any of this, Langston did." She shook her head slowly. "If anyone is to blame it's me. I'm the one who beat him up in the first place."

"You were having a hard time when the man put his hands on you." Josh shook his head. "He shouldn't have touched you at all."

"I'm just thankful we don't have to deal with him anymore." Frank said. "Not that I would wish death on anyone."

"We know you aren't that way Frank." Josh assured him. "I think it's time for us to get out of your hair. We have a honeymoon to get to."

"Congratulations you two." Ginger sniffed, "And thanks for the cake and champagne."

"You're welcome. You rest and get better." Jillian replied.

They waved goodbye to Frank as Josh backed out of the driveway looking forward to their two weeks away. The plan was to drive to Arkansas and honeymoon on their way there and back.

Leaving Wolf Creek behind for a few days was just what Josh needed. Having his new bride made it even more enjoyable. His only worry was what he would come back home to.

***

Frank tried one more time to call his sister. The voice mail reported it was full.

"Where are you Elysa? Why aren't you picking up?" he muttered to himself.

His gut feeling told him she was in trouble, but how do you look for someone who didn't tell you where they were going? He regretted the fight they'd had when he took her to the airport. She hugged him before she left on a flight to Houston with a stop in Denver. From there he had no idea where she and the reporter Marty Granger went.

Abe had been searching for her, but it seemed as though she had dropped off the face of the earth. He lost track of her in Denver, Colorado. According to the airport she never boarded the flight to Houston, Texas.

She left the number for Marty and when he called him, he had no idea where she was. He figured Frank had talked her out of the job, so he hired another photographer. The creep never even tried to contact anyone when she didn't show at the airport. Oh, he said he called her cell, but after several tries, he gave up.

Shadow knocked on the front door anxiously waiting for Frank to answer.

"Hey what's up?" Frank opened the door.

"Have you been able to reach her?" he asked.

"No, and Abe said she never made the connecting flight from Denver to Houston." Frank shook his head. "Her voicemail box is full."

"Send me to Denver. I'll track her down," he insisted.

"I'll send Justice with you since Hawk is still mad at you." Frank sighed wishing he could go himself. "I wanna go but with Ginger still recovering, I have to stay here."

"I'll find her." Shadow insisted.

"I'll have Barbara make the reservations and alert Justice." Frank said. "She'll call you when the arrangements have been made."

"Thanks, but I need Hawk instead. I know we still have issues, but I know his skills and he's the best other than me." Shadow relaxed a tiny bit. "Just so you are aware. When I find your sister, I'm gonna let her have it for not calling. Then I'm gonna take her on a date."

"I figured." Frank chuckled. "She might just take you up on that."

"I have your permission then?" Shadow grinned.

"Of course." Frank laughed. "I seem to remember you going through this with Star."

"Trace is a good honorable man. I'm pleased with her choice." Shadow said. "I'll go pack my things."

"Keep me in the loop." Frank said slapping his shoulder.

"I will." Shadow said as he stepped outside. "I'll see you when I get back with your sister."

Follow Shadow and Hawk in their quest to find
their boss's sister, Elysa Goines.
The answer to her disappearance will surprise
you.
Elysa's Savior coming soon.

I hope you enjoyed reading Josh's Dream. I
invite you take a few moments to submit a review
on Amazon.

Check out other books by R. .J.

Charlie's Park Bench
https://www.amazon.com/dp/B083RLPWHQ

Heroes of Wolf Creek series

Will's Heart
https://www.amazon.com/dp/B08HKNTLP7

Ginger's Hope
https://www.amazon.com/dp/B098R4HGC8

Trace's Star
https://www.amazon.com/gp/product/B0B5VT
LJHM

Made in the USA
Columbia, SC
10 March 2023